SPY VS. SPY

"Maybe we should go a few rounds—might be fun. You might find out the difference between a civilian and a pro," Special Agent Alex Scott suggested.

"I am a pro," pro boxer Kelly Robinson replied humorlessly. "These are lethal weapons, man. Don't screw with me."

Scott started circling him, hands assuming the blade-like form of the martial artist. "You've been trained to fight in a little square 'ring'— I've been trained to kill a man, anywhere . . . anytime. Want some, Champ?"

Circling too, fists up, Robinson said, "Don't do this, Alex . . ."

"Come on—it'll be amusing."

"If you think two weeks of dental work's amusing, yeah."

"Fair warning," Scott said, and he held up a thumb and forefinger. "I could kill you with these two fingers."

And the world middleweight champion threw a punch, lightning fast, connecting solidly with Scott's face.

I SPY

A novel by
Max Allan Collins
Based on the screenplay by
Cormac Wibberley & Marianne Wibberley
and
Jay Scherick & David Ronn

HarperEntertainment
An Imprint of HarperCollinsPublishers

HARPERENTERTAINMENT
An Imprint of HarperCollins*Publishers*
10 East 53rd Street
New York, New York 10022-5299

First HarperEntertainment paperback printing: October 2002

HarperCollins®, 🏛 ®, and HarperEntertainment™ are trademarks of HarperCollins Publishers Inc.

Printed in the United States of America

Visit HarperEntertainment on the World Wide Web at
www.harpercollins.com

10 9 8 7 6 5 4 3 2 1

For Albert Hickey
and
Franklin Boggs

"It was part of his profession to kill people. . . . Regret was unprofessional."

IAN FLEMING

I SPY

1

···

In the ivory glow of a full moon, the craggy gray-blue shapes of the Siberian mountains cut the sky like a half-finished jigsaw puzzle. Another shape, like a stray puzzle piece, hovered fifteen thousand feet above one slope: a high-altitude unmarked U.S. military helicopter, a Black Hawk, its blades a dark blur in the night, engine roar muffled to a purr, its side door sliding open to allow an anonymous figure to pitch purposefully out.

The covert agent—clad in goggles and a white snow-camo jumpsuit—had his booted feet in the bindings of a snowboard; in midair, there was no white stuff to traverse, merely a smoke-gray sky, but with acrobatic ease the agent navigated nothing, twirling in what might have seemed (had anyone been around to watch) a showboating display, and was in fact a skillful guidance of his trajectory. At one thousand feet, more or less, the agent yanked his ripcord to unleash a silken mushroom, and the rest of his descent was silent and less flashy . . . but precisely on target.

Alexander Scott—Alex or Scotty to his friends (only his mother used the longer formal form)—

waited until he was about twenty feet above the snowy slope, disengaged his parachute and dropped expertly onto the side of the mountain. Not missing a beat, Scott snowboarded down the steep grade, dodging rocky outcroppings and cutting between trees with a smooth powerful turn for every twist, and twist for every turn.

Alex Scott might have been a California surfer shooting the curl—and not just because of his mastery of the snowboard. He was a slender, deceptively muscular man in his late twenties, with the blond good looks of a Baywatch beach god, undermined slightly by a nose that had been broken so many times the memory of its original shape was distant indeed.

However much he might resemble a college student on a winter vacation—however laid-back and quirkily humorous his demeanor might seem—Scott was a highly trained agent, who had been with the CIA for several years before the BNS snatched him up. A Rhodes scholar, graduate of Temple, an accomplished linguist, Scott knew as many ways to kill a man (or a woman) as he did languages.

And Alex Scott knew a *lot* of languages.

Cutting a turn, he glided to a stop on a ridge to have a look below, where in an otherwise gloomy landscape a glow of illumination took centerstage. Under high bright lamps, behind ominous barbed wire, a silo rose like a middle finger taunting the agent, an igloo-like steelframe guard station connecting with this simple structure that had once housed a missile and now—if intelligence was to be believed—served as a marker of an underground complex used as one of those legendarily dire prisons for which Siberia was infamous.

In a silence broken only by the whisper of wind on snow, Scott studied the objective, mentally comparing it to satellite photos, going through the plan—which he had developed himself—for this rescue. Well, sort of rescue. . . .

He took a brief moment to prepare himself, and was just about to push off, when the nighttime silence was shattered by the ring of a cell phone.

Shit!

With all this planning, how could he have neglected to turn the damn thing off! This thought was streaking accusingly through his brain as he fumbled for the phone—he knew where every precious, sometimes deadly item was, in the many pockets on the jumpsuit . . . *except the damn cell*—and then he found it, and yanked it out, only to have his gloved hands fumble the thing. For a moment he juggled it, then dropped it again, and when he reached for it, the shifting of his weight at the edge of the ridge made the snow give way.

Which is how a brilliant, highly trained secret agent—impeccably prepared for this dangerous mission—came to fall ass over teakettle, tumbling down the slope until a pine tree was kind enough to stop him with a slam that sent snow from branches avalanching down on him, burying him . . .

. . . him, and the still ringing cell phone.

Scott pawed and powdered his way out from under the hill of snow. He was alive. He was fine. And that

phone was still trilling, like a small alarm in the stillness.

He slipped his left hand from its glove and thumbed
the cell, whispering harshly: "Hello."

"Mr. Scott," a pleasantly female young voice
chirped efficiently, "this is Charisse with Pro Hair Design—you missed your appointment this morning."

The wind flecked snow, mockingly, into Scott's
frustrated face. "I'm working!"

"If you reschedule now, Mr. Scott, we can avoid
your 'no show' penalty, and—"

"Clarise . . ."

"Charisse."

"Charisse, I'm cutting back on haircuts for a while."

"Then I'm afraid you will have to pay the—"

"No show fee, fine. I'm kinda working on a ponytail, here. . . ."

"Oh Mr. Scott," the young voice said chidingly,
"surely you know how out of style—"

"I kinda like out of style, Charisse . . . and you have
a nice voice, you really do. . . ." She really did. "But I
kinda gotta go right now."

And he thumbed END, and put his glove back on,
wondering if James Bond had ever had this problem.
Wondering, in fact, if James Bond ever even *needed* a
haircut. . . .

Within minutes, the jumpsuit, goggles and snow-
shoes had been abandoned behind a crest of snow, and
Alex Scott in a brown military uniform was standing
at the door of the fieldstone guard station—the only
entrance to the Siberian prison, save scaling the

barbed wire and maybe climbing that silo—where he knocked, firmly, confidently.

Within the cylindrical weathered-steel guardhouse, two sentries in khaki shirts hanging open over dark t-shirts were sleeping on the job. The smaller of the two, with a shaved head and a scraggly chin beard, slumped at a barrel that served as a makeshift table, where earlier the two had been playing cards. The taller guard—dark-haired, several days separating him from his last shave—reclined on a bench near more barrels in the open yet oddly claustrophobic space. The drab, rust-colored interior of the hut was sparsely furnished—a desk, a bench, and assorted kerosene heaters; the tunnel-shaped guardhouse provided a passage to the olive-green doors of a freight-style elevator.

Neither guard was in a deep sleep: these were just men whose jobs were so uneventful and possessed of so few duties that ennui had settled inevitably in. Their weapons were on this barrel and that one, the taller guard's Makarov pistol within its owner's reach, and the shorter, cueball-headed one's 5.45 millimeter AK-74 lay before him like stakes left over from the card game.

But the sharp knock at the door jarred them to alertness, scaring them a little—not a lot of visitors dropped by a prison in the Siberian mountains; traffic tended to be light.

Both grabbed their weapons, and the taller one rolled off his bench and ran to one of several windows, wiping a circle in the fogged-up pane, revealing the smiling blond countenance of a stranger in a familiar uniform . . .

. . . a stranger holding up two bottles of Stolichnaya vodka.

"Provisions are here!" the taller guard said in his native tongue, holstering his pistol, glancing back with a smile at his mate seated at the barrel.

The cueball guard knew what that meant: *Vodka!* Leaving his AK-74 behind, he strode to the door, opening it to let in their welcome guest, a supply officer who was two days early.

Alex Scott stepped into the pleasant, hearth-like warmth of the guard house, the taller guard shutting the door on the bitter cold, the cueball one grinning at the sight of the two Stoli bottles.

"Greetings, comrades," Scott said in perfectly accented Russian. He was a natural at foreign languages (at Temple, some had called him an idiot savant, but that was jealousy).

The tall one commented on the supply officer's early arrival, adding, "Not that we're complaining."

The other one inquired about the regular supply officer, saying, "Where is Ivan? We were hoping to take his money at cards."

"Ivan," Scott said, with a slightly frozen smile. "Well, you would not have heard."

The tall guard squinted. "Heard what, comrade?"

Scott shook his head, made a clicking sound in his cheek. "Poor old Ivan—he was mauled by a couple of the sled dogs."

The guard frowned. "How terrible."

Scott set the two bottles on the barrel-table, and shrugged fatalistically. "I told Ivan once if I told him a thousand times—using the whip like that was going to turn those pups against him."

"Interesting." The guard tilted his head, his eyes narrowing. "But what sled dogs are these? Ivan drives a truck."

Scott managed half a smile as he looked from one glowering Russian face to the other.

And in English he said, "Y'know, ever since the budget cuts, our intelligence has flat-out sucked."

The guards went for their guns—the tall one for his holstered Makarov, the shorter one for the AK-74 on the barrel; but the American agent was too fast for them. From under his brown khaki coat, he withdrew an oversize, vaguely futuristic pistol and fired twice . . .

. . . sending a tranquilizer dart into the chest of either man; stunned just long enough for the sedative to take hold, they collapsed unconscious to the cement.

Scott slipped the oversized tranq pistol into his holster beneath his coat, grabbed the two bottles off the barreltop, and headed for the elevator, which was behind a clear plexi door. He tried to slide it open, unsuccessfully, and soon realized that the damn thing was locked.

"Not a great start," he said to himself, in English, wishing he'd been kidding about the sucky intelligence of late.

On the desk he found a large ring of keys, presenting at least fifty possibilities. He did not feel like working his way through the whole half hundred, so he reluctantly returned to the cueball guard, withdrew from a pocket a disposable syringe and jammed it into the man's chest.

The adrenaline surge sat the guard bolt upright, and he blinked at Scott, who was dangling the ring of many keys before him, like a hypnotist's watch.

"Comrade," Scott said in the guard's language, "which key? Which *key?*"

The guard raised an unsure hand to his chest, just above where the dart still stuck out, like a ghastly corsage; then the man's thick fingers fumbled up to his neck, where he slowly fished free a chain on which hung a single key.

"*That's* the key?"

The guard bobbled his head.

"That's ridiculous." Scott shook the fat ring of keys. "What are all of these for?"

Dazed, disoriented, the Russian stared at the American, apparently not sure himself. Then he managed, "Decoy?"

Suddenly understanding why Uncle Sam had won the cold war, Scott stood and withdrew the tranq pistol again and shot another dart into the guard, who promptly passed back out. He wasn't sure the double dose wouldn't kill the man, but Scott—off the job, a decent, moral guy—had been trained in the necessary amorality of his work.

As the rickety, open elevator lowered him to the prison level, Scott knew (or *hoped* he knew) from intelligence that only another two guards would be waiting. But again, that data proved flawed: a half dozen guards—these looking more soldierly in their khakis and garrison caps—were apparently preparing for the next Olympics, playing a rough, rowdy game of basketball in the large, open, silo-like space.

The game progressed, the three-on-three paying no heed to his arrival, until a beaming Scott walked up to them, holding up a bottle of Stoli in either hand, saying in Russian, "Supplies, comrades! Fresh supplies!"

The half dozen basketball stars forgot the game and—with child-like exclamations of "Vodka! Vodka!"—met Scott half-way.

"Ivan is back in the truck," Scott said, anticipating their first question.

But there were no questions at all, actually, the first two guards grabbing the bottles of Stoli and the others standing before Scott with the glittering hard-eyed expressions of wolfhounds expecting a biscuit . . . and ready to tear into his flesh if they didn't get one.

"Ah," Scott said. "Yes . . . I would not neglect my comrades. . . ."

And Scott was indeed prepared, even in the face of poor intelligence; from yet another pocket he withdrew miniature airline-style bottles of Stoli, which he passed out to the smiling Russians, who immediately began twisting off the tiny caps and taking the vodka like medicine.

The American agent sized the group up, and one of the two who had come forward and taken the larger bottles . . . in fact, the tall Dolph Lundgren clone who'd snatched the first of the bottles . . . seemed obviously in charge.

So Scott approached the bare-headed, muscular apparition and said, "Moscow wants a picture of the American."

"A picture?"

The affable agent withdrew a small disposable camera of Russian make, or at least so it appeared. "Apparently a trade is in the offing. But ours is not to reason why, eh, comrade?"

"That much," the brawny guard allowed, "never changes."

"And I have to speak to him . . . in private. Ask designated questions . . . though I myself do not understand their significance."

This, too, made sense to the guard.

Soon Scott was being led down a cylindrical corridor, sorry cells on either side, filthy underfed bearded inmates within, the floor damp, the air fetid, pools of light from small overhead lamps doing little to fend off the gloom. For a moment Alexander Scott—his and the guard's footsteps echoing off the moist cement like hollow gunshots—pondered just how very hard he had worked to get inside this hellhole where inmates dreamed vainly of getting out.

About half-way down the protracted corridor, the guard stopped, indicated a cell, which he unlocked and opened; then the guard did Scott a favor and marched back down the tunnel, leaving the secret agent alone with the prisoner, a fact underscored by the ominous echoing click of the main cellblock gate.

In the far corner of the dank, unlighted cell—a single cot and a seatless toilet made up the less-is-more decor—huddled a brown-haired American in green khakis; having no reason to think Scott was anything but another Russian, the prisoner—his face bruised and puffy from countless beatings—turned away from his unwanted visitor.

Scott knelt beside the man and spoke in a hushed tone . . . in English. "Lieutenant John Percy?"

The prisoner turned toward his visitor now, hope glimmering in the swollen eyes, the dirty, bearded face alive suddenly, with relief. "Thank God," he breathed.

Lt. Percy got to his feet, glanced toward the half-open barred door which led only to a locked cell block; then he faced his potential savior. "You've got to get my ass out of here—I can't live through many more of these damn beatings."

Scott stood with his arms folded. His expression was bereft of sympathy when he said, "And where's the plane, John?"

"The plane? The plane?"

"Does this look like Fantasy Island, John? Where is the plane?"

The cell door at his back, Percy said, "I flamed out. Had to ditch."

"Ah."

"It's at the bottom of the Caspian Sea."

"Caspian Sea. Did you know that's where the legend of the mermaid began?"

The pilot's eyes tensed, confused by the offhanded demeanor of the American agent. "Uh, no . . . what?"

"And I guess it was a mermaid who turned off the recovery beacon, 'cause you sure wouldn't . . . right? You holding up okay? Anything I can get you?"

"Get me out of here."

"Pretty rough on you, gettin' shot down over Russian airspace in an unmarked Cessna. How much cash was in that suitcase your hosts confiscated? Our intelligence doesn't say . . . 'course intel's been sucky lately."

Percy approached Scott, who was casually popping a wad of gum in his mouth. "Just get me out of here and I'll tell you everything."

"I'm sure it'll be an intriguing tale . . . but what I want to know . . . what I need to know . . . is *where is the Switchblade?*"

That was the name of the top-secret plane, in Percy's care, which had gone missing.

Percy almost smiled, though with that battered face it was hard to tell. "Get me out and I'll tell you," he said.

"Hmmm," Scott said, chewing. "I don't think so."

"Listen carefully, clown," Percy said, frustration and panic combining in a desperate toughness. "I'm not saying one word until you get my ass *out* of here."

Scott seemed to consider that for a moment, then said, "All right . . . tell you what. I'm gonna go—this place gets me down. Very negative energy. . . . Maybe I'll stop by again, in a few weeks. Maybe you'll feel more like talking, then."

Scott exited the cell, leaving the door slightly ajar; and he started back down the tunnel-like corridor, his feet making their little gunshot echoes on the wet cement.

Percy was at the cell door, yelling, his voice reverberating, "You can't leave me here! I'm an American citizen!"

But this was Russia, and the words were both hollow and foreign, to these walls.

And Alexander Scott kept walking, heading toward the cellblock door.

"Okay!" Percy's voice echoed behind him. "Gundars! I sold the plane to Arnold goddamn Gundars!"

At last, Scott thought, still walking, *intelligence had been right about something.*

The pilot's voice continued to reverberate behind Scott: "I swear to God! That's the truth! It *is* the truth!"

By this time Scott was at the cellblock door. From Percy's unenviable perch, Scott surely seemed about to leave; but instead he removed the wad of gum from his mouth and stuffed it into the keyhole of the cellblock door, fitting it there as if he were puttying up a bad patch in plaster. A pair of cellblock guards—nearby, but not on top of this—watched in bemusement.

Scott gave them a smile, a nod, said, "Comrades," and turned to walk back toward the pilot's cell.

"Is there a problem?" a guard called out in Russian, from the other side of the cellblock door.

The American agent turned, shook his head, and waved.

And now the guard knew something was up, something was *wrong,* and he attempted to unlock the cell-block . . .

. . . but when the guard inserted his key into that gummed-up keyhole, the substance solidified, tightening onto, containing, swallowing the key, blocking it from turning in the lock.

As the guard urgently called out to his fellows, Scott hurried back to Percy's cell, where the pilot realized a rescue indeed was under way, though he was as confused as that main gate sentry.

"Did I just see you lock us in?" the prisoner asked.

"Rule number one," Scott said, stepping back into the cell. " 'Never enter a site unless you've got a sure way out.' "

From a pocket Scott withdrew the small disposable camera, off of which he removed the back panel of paper, revealing a glistening sticky pad. The waste paper he stuck to the lock mechanism, to keep the cell door open and unlocked, should the facility have a remote switch.

The agent slammed the sticky side of the "camera" to the ceiling of the cell, pressing down on the shutter button, engaging the device, which began to beep in a countdown that Scott kept track of even as he yanked the pilot by the arm and from the cell and into the corridor, out of harm's way.

Percy looked at him, bewildered, and Scott said, "Say cheese," and the device exploded, a massive detonation that sent smoke and debris raining sideways into the hall.

But Scott and the pilot ran right into the billowing

aftermath of the blast, back into the cell to make their exit out of the hole the agent had just blown in the ceiling . . .

. . . except the hole didn't lead anywhere. It wasn't really a hole at all, just a crater in concrete that provided no passage at all.

The pilot whirled to the agent, his eyes wide and wild. "That's it? Rule number one? Your 'sure' way out?"

"Did I mention intelligence sucked lately?"

The din of more guards, thankfully still well down the corridor, behind the locked cellblock door, echoed threateningly toward them.

Percy glared accusingly at Scott. "You wouldn't happen to have a 'rule number two' up your sleeve, I suppose?"

"General rule," Scott said. "Shut up and run."

Again he grabbed the pilot by the sleeve, and hauled him out into the corridor, where gunshots sought them through the bars of that locked cellblock door, bullets *whing*ing and *whang*ing off the steel walls, all around them.

They came to where the corridor deadended—at least they were out of pistol range now, until the guards got that barred door open anyway—and Scott looked up, hoping the information about the prison's layout was right in this respect, and it was: above him, as promised, was a ventilation grate, a beautiful gridwork square in the steel ceiling.

Scott jumped up and grabbed onto an overhead pipe and swung his booted feet up, kicking the vent in with a solid satisfying metallic crunch. Then he dropped back onto the floor, made a step out of his interlaced fingers to give Percy a boost up into the shaft; the pilot reached a hand down and helped Scott climb in after.

The vent led up into the warmth of a small dreary area taken up primarily by an old-fashioned boiler. Percy replaced the slightly dented vent grate, in hopes of camouflaging their escape route; but pounding feet and frantic shouting seeped up from below . . . indicating the cellblock door had finally been breached.

"We are so dead," Percy whispered.

"Would you *please* stop being so negative," Scott said offhandedly, as he quickly scanned the small steel room, noting a duct that rose from the boiler into the ceiling, and a stoking shovel leaning against one wall. A door in the chamber seemed promising, and it was unlocked; but cracking it open let in the sounds of guards—distant, but not *that* distant. . . .

And below, in the tunnel-like corridor, guards were streaming in and down, and soon were at the deadend, milling around under the grating.

Scott heard a radio clicking on and a voice, in Russian, crisply stating, "They are in the boiler room."

The agent tossed a handgun to the pilot, a Russian PMM, and told him to cover the boiler-room door.

Cautiously opening it, the pilot peeked out, but the sounds of guards—voices and footsteps—were much louder now, and he shut it again, quickly.

"Watch your back," Scott advised, and Percy whirled and just managed to jump out of the way, as the boiler duct—freed by Scott using the stoking shovel—came rattling down, stopping with a crash, even as steam rushed out from the boiler where the duct had connected.

The vent fell across the grate in the floor that had been their entry into the boiler room—blocking that from the guards below—and jammed itself against the chamber's door, wedging it nicely, tightly, shut.

"Rule number two," Percy said, impressed, "must be 'improvise.'"

Grabbing a wheel on the boiler and cranking it, shutting off a valve, Scott said, "Rule number two is 'Stay positive.'"

The agent glanced at the boiler's pressure gauge; the result would be the intended one. . . .

"Come on!" Scott said, gesturing to the fresh opening in the ceiling, where the duct had formerly connected. This time the agent went first, the pilot pausing to consider his options—the floor grate, under the fallen duct, was pulsing with the efforts of the Russians below, trying to lift it; and the blocked door was being battered and banged against.

The pilot jumped up into the air shaft.

The vent was maybe thirty inches wide and went straight up, like a chimney; Scott made his way up by wedging his back against one side, and his feet on the other. The pilot followed suit, a painfully slow, inefficient process . . . but the only one available.

As the secret agent and the renegade pilot exercised this peculiar sort of shinnying, the Russian guards below were doing their best to get into the boiler room, unaware that steam was building up perilously, no one to see the pressure gauge revealing the swelling steam sending the needle into the red zone . . . nor to see the steam shooting out of every nook and cranny on the boiler, desperately seeking escape . . .

. . . much like Scott and Percy, who were perhaps a third of the way up that seemingly never-ending shaft. That steam was fleeing far quicker than the two Americans, seeping up around them, heating their vertical world, the two men drenched, dripping with sweat.

Two groups of Russians attempted to storm the small bastion that the boiler room had, in their minds, become . . . unaware they were working so hard, so desperately, to gain passage into a virtual bomb.

One group, in the hallway outside the boiler room, used gun butts, inserting them like levers into the door, which they'd gotten open just enough to do that, huffing, grunting, swearing in Russian, using words and phrases even an expert linguist like Alexander Scott might not recognize.

The other group had enterprisingly formed a human pyramid of themselves, under the grating at the dead-end of the cellblock corridor, below the boiler room, and were pushing up, the top guard jammed unforgivingly against the metal grate . . . and here too some vivid Russian swearing was disbursed, Alex Scott denied the pleasure of these vivid, earthy phrases.

The guard squashed against the grating put his back and shoulders and arms into it, and helped lift the gridwork up enough to get a small look around . . .

. . . and he was the first to realize what a fool's errand they were all on, seeing the needle pinned into the red on the boiler's pressure gauge, the boiler itself having a nervous breakdown, shaking, shivering, shimmying, shrieking in apparent pain, steam shooting out everywhere.

The guard shrieked, too, and didn't take the time to swear, either: "Let me down! Get back! Let me down!"

Half-way up the vent shaft, Scott and Percy could hear the high-pitched whistling, increasing in volume, climbing in pitch, and the amount of steam finding its nasty way up to them had increased, as well.

The Americans doubled their efforts to get the hell out, and Percy lost his sideways footing for a moment, Scott reaching down to grab his hand, and brace him.

The pilot—who had long since forgotten about suitcases of cash, and a new affluent life—gazed up at his rescuer with raw gratitude.

"Stay positive," Scott advised, barely audible over the scream of steam, and their ascent continued.

That was when the bomb that the boiler had become blew itself into shrapnel.

The guards in the hallway finally got that door open, but they had nothing to do with it: the blast blew it back on them, carrying them, shooting them down the hall and into a wall with an awful bone-breaking thud.

And the guards below the grating, who had frantically been trying to dissemble their acrobat's pyramid, were blown to the floor in a carelessly strewn pile by the explosive gust of smoke and steel.

Outside the prison, the world seemed a peaceful place, washed in ivory moonlight, the wind whispering, a slumbering, snowy landscape marred only the barbed wire fence and the stark former missile silo. Into this stillness, through a vent hiding in the snow, came blasting out two human cannonballs—Scott and Percy—making the last third of their passage in much better time.

Flung to the snow, cushioned there, the two men examined themselves quickly—limbs, eyes intact, not hurt at all really, merely stunned. But they had landed (on the better side of the fence at least) not far from the metal igloo guardhouse where the fun had all begun, and they did not have time to even brush the white off themselves before guards with rifles—AKSU-74s—and submachine guns—Stechkin APS's—came streaming out, their breath pluming, their eyes wild and angry.

Scott was first on his feet, and once again he yanked the pilot by the arm, and gestured with a head bob toward the woods at the mountain's base. Then both men were scrambling through the snow, making for the trees and a rendezvous point known only to the secret agent.

With themselves and their pursuers both on foot, the chances of the prisoners would have seemed excellent—they had a good head start; but then Scott heard the mechanical growl, the rumble of snowmobiles, and knew their odds had just lessened.

A dozen guards on a dozen snowmobiles, headlights and flashlights crisscrossing the trees and brush, raced into the woods, seeking the escaped pilot and his would-be rescuer. Gunfire snapped at the night, chewed up the silence, as the angry staff of the prison sought revenge for the humiliation these two had brought down upon them; every shadow, every moon-lit reflection, brought a response, as firearms punched holes in Russian air and Siberian trees and sought better purchase in American flesh.

Scott stopped to lean against a tree, not so much to catch his breath, but to try to get better oriented; Percy stood, leaning, hands on his knees, Russian pistol in one hand, breathing hard. The secret agent had long since wandered from any semblance of the original plan, and any Plan B, in fact the entire damn alphabet, was at this point moot.

Shots kicked at snow nearby, pretty little puffs of white that sent Scott and Percy scurrying behind the thick trunk of a tree.

"I know you've been in an underground prison lately," Scott said conversationally, glancing around. "But you wouldn't happen to remember, from when they brought you here, which way the sun sets?"

The pilot seemed to be thinking about that, but then brought up the Makarov and leveled it, chest high, at the secret agent.

"It sets behind me?" Scott said, as if that was why the pistol was aimed at him.

"I didn't get out of that hellhole," Percy said, his voice a low growl not unlike that of the pursuing snowmobiles, "just to land my ass back in prison in the States."

"I shouldn't have given you that gun," Scott said, with a shrug and a smile. "See, there's such a thing as being *too* positive. . . ."

The pilot's expression might have been that of a man smelling something very foul. "How did you *get* this job?"

"Thing is, I'm too trusting. People always tell me that, and I just never listen."

Lulled by the casualness of the spy's words, and by his laid-back demeanor, the pilot was not ready for Scott—who, in a move so quick it almost seemed not to have happened, grabbed the gun, twisted it free, and resumed control.

"I'd rather not kill you," Scott said. That was true, but then part of his mission was to bring this traitor back alive; so it wasn't just that he was a nice guy. . . .

Another series of shots rippled through the night, close to them—too damn close, a slug catching Percy in the hip. The pilot dropped to the snow, crying out, "I'm hit!"

"Serves you right," Scott said, "using my gun on me."

Nonetheless, the secret agent bent down, picked up the pilot and slung him over his shoulder, Marines-style, and took off at a half-jog, as gunfire popped and ripped all around them. Scott wove in and around trees, choosing a thick patch, increasing his chances; wood flew around them, splinters careening into the night, as bullets whined and thunked and cracked.

Somehow, somewhere in that forest, carrying the traitor on his back, Alexander Scott got his bearings;

or perhaps the Russians had just inadvertently driven him in the right direction. At any rate, a familiar engine sound, distinct from that of the snowmobiles, soon confirmed his instincts . . . and within minutes Scott and his burden were at the clearing, where the Black Hawk helicopter waited, hovering fifteen feet off the open ground, rotors whirling and whirring, a sound so reassuring Scott couldn't keep the silly grin off his face.

The grin didn't last long—the snow here was deep, thigh-high, and though the night was bitterly cold, sweat poured down his face, cheeks crimson with the effort, a man at the end of a marathon, seeking that elusive finishing-line ribbon, so close, so distant. The bullets were dancing in the snow behind him—he was just out of range, or at the edge of it, and he did his best to run, despite the heaviness of the man on his shoulders. His legs ached, muscles burned, but he pressed on.

The Black Hawk was laying down cover for them, keeping the Russians back just enough to give Scott and Percy a fighting chance. The powerful ordnance chewed up the forest, upending trees, the woods exploding, sending the Russians diving for cover.

The last few steps to the copter were free of Russian gunfire, and Scott set the pilot down in the open bay windows, about to climb up and in himself when the pilot looked at him stupidly wide-eyed, openmouthed.

"What?" Scott said, irritated with this S.O.B. "Get in! I saved your ass."

But, actually, Scott hadn't: the pilot pitched forward like a rag doll off its shelf; the man's back was stitched with bullet holes, red kisses on khaki.

"All right," Scott said with a sigh, thinking how hard it was to stay positive, sometimes. "This is like . . . the worst day—*ever*."

Now the bullets started up again, the Russians peppering the copter around him, metal on metal making its discordant music. So Scott dove head first into the bay door, just as the copter lifted off. The Black Hawk banked into a turn, and whisked away into the gray sky.

Scott had retrieved Lt. Percy, but the dead man wouldn't provide much of a debriefing for the secret agent's superiors. He could only hope Percy hadn't been lying about Arnold Gundars; that scrap of information was all he had to show for tonight's mission.

And sometimes Mac—McIntyre, the head of the BNS—could get a little irritated with Scott.

Like when he brought home somebody he'd rescued who was kind of . . . dead.

2

Caesar never had a palace to rival the one in Las Vegas, Nevada, nor had he a coliseum to compare with the smoke-swirled arena where fifteen thousand-plus sports fans had gathered to watch gladiators in gloves. Screams and cheers echoed like happy decadent thunder through a darkness broken by banks of red-white-and-blue lighting, to help the cable TV cameras capture the carnage . . . that is, the sport . . . of a World Boxing Federation championship fight.

Two men brawled in this square ring, each a professional trained to batter the likes of the other, skilled at blotting out the crowd and the blue electric CAESAR'S PALACE banners and the carnival atmosphere, and hone in on each other's strengths . . . and weaknesses.

In purple trunks complementing his muscle-rippling frame, Blake Lirette—they called him the Blade (actually, he had called himself that, and "they" had gone along with him)—had the look of a street tough with his intense scowl. Barely past twenty, he bore the determined cast of an underdog taking on a champion . . . which was exactly the case.

Blake was facing off against Kelly Robinson—at

thirty-six, a modern legend, a latterday Ali, muscular
but not bulked up, a sinewy, balletically graceful
fighter with a handsome, trimly mustached oval countenance that looked as if it had never kissed a glove.
His black knee-length trunks, bearing the bold in-
signia KELLY (as if anyone needed help knowing
who this was), were adorned with the insignias of the
various boxing associations of which he held the
middleweight championship.

Descending Kelly Robinson's right arm from the
shoulder down his bicep and beyond were eleven
groups of four vertical lines with a fifth slanted
through it—as if a prisoner were marking off days in
sets of five. Below these simple, well-executed but
oddly undecorative tattoos, another vertical line indicated the beginning of another group of five. His left
arm was bare of any such . . . of *any* . . . tattoo. The
meaning of this was well-known to all those who followed the fight game; nonetheless, the champ usually
picked a key moment to explain to an opponent the
precise meaning of the unostentatious tattoos. . . .

Right now the audience was on its feet as the two
men fearlessly exchanged powerful combinations,
sweat flying (but not blood, not yet), as their red
gloves flashed in center ring, blows landing, neither
man seeming to feel a damn thing.

Light reflecting off the hills and valleys of his glistening milk-chocolate skin, Robinson danced away,
grinning, hands low, seemingly inviting the fiercely
focused White Hope to have another try.

"That all you got?" Robinson mocked, in his best

Cassius Clay manner. Speed, grace and trash-talking were his specialties. Psychological warfare was Kelly Robinson's favorite kind. "Your sister kisses harder than you punch."

As Robinson danced, the Blade moved in, staying low, making a small target of himself, the taunting tone of his opponent making no apparent inroad on the challenger's concentration.

Loosey goosey, Robinson pranced and moved his gloved hands as if trying to decide which to use. "All right, baby . . . here it comes. Left, right, left . . . you ready?"

Blake said nothing.

Robinson shrugged, then charged in, delivering a lightning left-right-left combo, scoring cleanly . . . and danced away.

It was clear the younger opponent had felt the blows, this time; and the ring announcers were going wild. . . .

"Unbelievable! Will you look at that!"

"The Champ has still *got the fastest hands in the sport!"*

But Kelly Robinson, behind his confident, cocky grin, was wondering why those blows hadn't taken more of a toll. He didn't let on, though, and the Ali mockery continued.

"Y'see," Robinson said, circling his opponent, "I call that combination the faze 'em, daze 'em and amaze 'em."

But Blake, moving with the champ like a cobra following his master's flute, slitted eyes like a snake's above poised red gloves, seemed unimpressed.

"It's on my website," Robinson said, still circling, his tone teasingly friendly. "You should check it out."

Blake's gloves lowered just a hair, and he spoke for the first time since they'd entered the ring: "Download this, old man. . . ."

And the young challenger attacked.

The combination wasn't as graceful as the one Robinson had delivered, but it contained twice as many blows, twice as hard, rocking, rattling the champ. The punishment was continuing when the bell rang and the ref pulled the duo apart.

It took all Robinson's will to walk cool and confident to his corner, to let the crowd—and more importantly, Blake—know that he had only been momentarily thrown by the blitz. Nonetheless, the ring announcers saw chinks in his armor. . . .

"That last combination really stung *the champ!"*

"I should say, Bob, it's obvious young Lirette's not about to roll over for Kelly Robinson."

Sitting heavily on his stool, Robinson spat out his mouthguard and spoke to his cornerman, Darryl, a small slender black man with a shaved head, a yellow KELLY ROBINSON jersey and a long history with the champ.

"This kid is tough as a two-buck t-bone," Robinson admitted.

Moving in with a towel, Darryl shrugged that off. "You beat his daddy—twice."

Robinson glared across the ring at his seated opponent, who seemed cool, not breathing hard. "Need more sex education in the schools."

Darryl blinked, like he thought his man had maybe taken a hard blow to the skull. "What, Champ?"

"People havin' babies *too* damn early. . . ."

The first half of the next round showed caution on the part of both boxers: each had given the other some of their best shit, and yet neither man had shown the other any sign of being bothered. Tiny flurries from both fighters amounted to little, and the crowd was getting surly.

Robinson generally ignored the crowd—what some perceived as showmanship was actually the psychological warfare that the champ felt was his real secret weapon—and some after-fight commentators would misinterpret what followed as showboating, a response to an audience whose boredom had become palpable.

Nonetheless, it was the Blade who made the first move, coming after Robinson, barely missing with several powerful blows, the champ responding, the end result a bear hug Robinson resorted to . . . not to catch his breath, but to resume his favorite form of combat.

"Blake," Robinson said, still locked in an embrace with his opponent, "that redhead in the second row. . . . That your lady?"

Blake struggled to break free—this innocuous remark had landed the best blow of the battle so far.

"Very pretty girl," Robinson said, not ready to let go of his opponent, either physically or psychologically. "Very pretty. . . ."

Blake pulled free, and Robinson threw a few playful, almost kidding jabs, both physical and verbal, including, "You think she'll have any hard feelings?"

The young challenger's frown said that he didn't understand.

"What I mean is . . . you think she'd have a drink with me tonight? So somebody can keep her company. . . . While you're in the hospital?"

Furious, Blake attacked with a vicious but undisciplined right cross, which Robinson dodged, no trouble, to counter with a less powerful but beautifully executed, and swift as hell, combination, sending Lirette stumbling backward into the ropes, like a drunk who tumbled off a high bar stool.

Now the ringside boys were back on the champ's side. . . .

"A devastating combination from the champ, and Lirette is stunned!"

"Bob, that's the Kelly Robinson we remember, the man we all came to see—that scientific boxing skill is why the man has never lost a fight, from the Olympics so many years ago to Caesar's Palace tonight!"

Robinson knew he could have moved in and finished off the staggered boxer—but he had his reasons not to, instead dancing around his wounded prey, gesturing to his strangely tattooed right shoulder with his fat padded glove.

"See that, Blake? Fifty-six . . ."

And now Robinson gestured to his left arm, bereft of tattoo.

". . . and oh. Five-six and oh. Which adds up to: you ain't got a prayer. Kelly R can't be beat."

The bell dinged, and—as Blake Lirette lurched to his corner—the champion strode to his, confident, cool, and cocky as ever . . . the crowd going berserk, a din the ring announcers had to work over to be heard.

"Another impressive round for Kelly Robinson!"

"You folks at home, you're watching boxing history in the making here . . . as Kelly Robinson will attempt to defend his title twice *in the same week. . . . Tonight, here in Vegas, and this coming Thursday in Budapest, where he faces Hungarian champ, Cedric Mills."*

"Bob, he's calling it—now I want to get this exactly right, or the champ'll be after my *hide—the 'Intercontinental, Super Punch-adental, Champion of the World Tour!"*

"Easy for you to say!"

Jerry—Robinson's burly, bald, bearded black trainer, a water jug in one hand, a jar of Vaseline in the other—leaned in and smeared some of the contents of the jar on the champ's face.

"Whoa, whoa, whoa, Guccione!" Robinson said, backing away. "Save that for the camera lens, when you're shootin' your ladies."

Darryl handed the champ a towel.

Robinson shot a look at Jerry, who held the Vaseline jar, chagrined. "I want to be shiny," the champ said, "not lumpy."

Another of his ring men—wiry T.J., like Darryl, a longtime Robinson aide-de-camp—leaned in and attended to his boss . . . and friend, saying, "You had him, Kel—why didn't you put him out of his misery?"

"T.J., do you know what tonight is?"

"Hell, Kel--it's the championship of the world!"

"It's the season finale of *Sopranos*. Check your watch—it don't end for another five minutes."

"You all right? You need the doc?"

Ignoring that, Robinson continued: "Which means, in five minutes, we get another million or so souls, tunin' in to watch me knock that Blade outta his razor."

T.J. was considering that when Robinson patted him on the head with a padded red glove.

"Think, T.J.," Robinson said. "Think . . . it's show business. . . ."

Shapely, skimpily-clad young women were holding up cards that read ROUND 3 as they circled the ring.

"Right, boss," T.J. said, "but now it's show-*time.* . . ."

The bell rang, and the champ went back out there, and for two rounds he danced and weaved and bobbed and mocked, occasionally landing a blow, continually infuriating Lirette, delighting the crowd, though the ringside commentators caught on.

"The Champ's just toying with him now, Bob."

"I'd almost say Robinson is prolonging this, just to put on a better show . . . but it's a dangerous game. Our young Blade will only put up with so much cutting up."

In the fifth round—well after *The Sopranos* had ended—Kelly Robinson cut the comedy and landed a solid right in the challenger's jaw, sweat flying off the younger man's head and hair like a small squall. It was almost enough to end the charade, but—as the ring announcers had predicted—Blake "the Blade" Lirette was not to be underestimated: he held on, and in fact came back immediately with a flurry of shots, any one of which could have dropped a building.

But Robinson evaded each and every blow, ducking, dodging, and—most humiliating of all, for the younger man—the champ kept his hands down at his sides, his face, his torso, unguarded, as if he couldn't be bothered with protecting himself from such a trifling opponent.

And when the challenger's flurry of missed opportunities ended, Kelly Robinson—at will—stepped in and landed a punishing left against the side of the young boxer's jaw, staggering him back.

The champ zeroed in for the kill, tensing, though his voice remained lightly mocking: "Here it comes, baby—here comes the night! The long, the lonely night . . . the big one. I call this one the 'Betcha goin' out on a Strecha' . . . s'on the website."

Fist cocked, Robinson moved in, but Lirette was the one dancing now—not gracefully, a shuffle to safety—and every time the champ would come at him, the challenger would retreat, and if this kept up, the bell would ring, and Lirette would catch his breath, get a second wind maybe, and Robinson'd have to start all over again.

So, fed up, the champ stopped.

And strode to the center of the ring.

The crowd went eerily quiet—not pin-drop so, that was impossible; but damn quiet, and every eye was wide and affixed on the center-ring champ . . . including those of Blake Lirette.

"All right," Robinson said. "I ain't chasin' you no more. This ain't track! . . . Come on, Blade—give ya a free shot at this beautiful face. You can be the first to lay a glove on it. . . ."

And Kelly Robinson dropped his hands to his sides . . . and closed his eyes.

"Robinson's eyes are shut!"

"Bob, I've never seen anything like this! He's daring Lirette to step up and clock him!"

The challenger did not move immediately in—he was studying the champ, unsure, Elmer Fudd expecting the worst from Bugs Bunny.

Robinson waited—his eyes seemed shut, though truth be told they were slitted just enough—and he began to sway his head, his whole upper body, like Stevie Wonder at the microphone.

"Come on, man! I can't see your ass! Where you at?"

In the champ's corner, his crew was apoplectic, the massive Jerry in particular, saying, "You open your damn eyes, Kelly Robinson, or I'm gonna come out there and pop you my own damn self!"

Now Robinson wasn't just swaying like Stevie Wonder; he was singing like him, too: " *'Isn't she lovely. . . . Isn't she won-der-ful. . . .'* Dreamin' about that redhead of yours, Blake. . . ."

The arena was a mass of jeering spectators now, humiliating Lirette, giving him no choice; quickly, silently, he moved in and threw a hard right hand . . .

. . . and Kelly Robinson—eyes not widening a sliver—slipped the punch and fired off his own right hand, catching the challenger on the chin with an explosive, vicious blow that sent the young man, and all his hopes and dreams of glory, crashing to the canvas in a splash of sweat, saliva and blood.

The crowd was on its collective feet, their roar enough to raise the roof . . . but not to rouse Blake "the Blade" Lirette.

The ref counted over Lirette, as Robinson—serious, almost somber, the mocking over now—strode coolly to his corner and the smiles and pats-on-the-back from all his corner crew, disciples who had doubted and denied him.

A little more than an hour later—after a quick press conference and a lingering shower—Kelly Robinson and his entourage were in a cordoned-off area of one of the casino's several nightclubs. A live band on a stage across the way was playing vintage soul tunes, instrumental arrangements—right now, a James Brown medley.

Robinson and his posse sat at a cluster of small tables, at one of which the champ—his shirt off—was having another line added to his right-arm tattoo. A beautiful black woman of perhaps twenty-three, in a postage stamp cocktail dress, was standing behind him, rubbing the champ's shoulders, taking his mind off the pain.

Not that he was feeling any. The champ did not hide his smugness; he even reveled in it, as he said, "Fifty-seven and oh . . . and two days from now, fifty-eight and oh. Man, you might just as well put a damn *infinity* sign there, 'cause I ain't *never* goin' down!"

The beauty rubbing Robinson's neck said, "Don't be so sure!"

Laughter followed that.

"Well," Robinson said, flashing the toothiest grin on the planet, "let's just say I ain't never gonna *lose*."

Whoops and claps affirmed that, and Darryl, seated nearby, redundantly added, "Straight up, Boss. . . . Only, you don't retire undefeated pretty soon, you're gonna run out of space on that arm. Where you gonna put those marks after that?"

Another female voice from the rear called out: "I can think of someplace!"

More laughter, and a few whoops, ensued, and Darryl was grinning, too, proud of himself.

Robinson leaned in to the man and said pleasantly, "Darryl, you been with me, what? Ten years?"

"Ten years, Kel. Ten sweet years."

"That's right. You my boy—that's established. So you can get your head outa my ass now. . . . Check with Jerry if you need a little Vaseline."

Another ripple of laughter was punctuated by T.J. saying, "Seriously, Darryl. This kiss-ass, it's pathetic."

Robinson said, "T.J.—you only been with me for *three* years. You keep your head where it's at."

T.J. shrugged. "I'm cool with that."

The living doll stopped rubbing the champ's shoulders, now that the tattoo artist was finished and had slipped away; she drew close and began to nibble on Robinson's ear, saying, "You are sooooo strong, Kelly."

Robinson smiled at her, no teeth this time. "I like

the way you say my name, girl. Kinda rolls off your tongue: Kelllly."

She giggled, nibbled, said, "Kelllly. . . ."

"Yeah . . . just like that." Then he pulled away, just a little, just enough to look right at her. "You should know that you are very, very close."

She frowned, barely. "Say what?"

"Very close to coming home with me tonight."

The frown vanished, a tiny smile curled. "I'd like that."

"Yes you would," Robinson said, with utter confidence. "But, uh. . . . I don't know. I just need a little somethin' more, to help me . . . you know . . . decide."

"Decide?"

"Maybe you should run over to the bar and write a little essay for me."

"Essay what?"

"You can call it, 'Why it would not be a waste of his valuable time for Kelly Robinson to spend the night with me.' By whatever-your-name-is."

"Lateesha." She was frowning again, obviously not sure if he was kidding.

"That's fine. Now, Lateesha, grab yourself some cocktail napkins, and maybe get your lipstick outa your purse, and start writing. Kinda like a . . . pop quiz. You got fifteen minutes."

She moved away from him, thinking—Robinson wasn't sure if she was taking him up on his fool's errand, or stalking out; but nonetheless he rubbed a little salt in the wound: "And don't you be cheatin' off that blond bitch, neither."

Around him, his guys were shaking their heads and smiling; and then a cell phone trilled, and Darryl reached into his jacket and answered the call.

"Yeah," Darryl said, and a few moments later, he jerked straight in his seat, as if a teacher had corrected him. "Yes, sir! Thank you. . . . Hold on, sir, please. Thank you!"

Robinson looked at Darryl as if the man had lost his mind—the rest of the crew was doing likewise—but Darryl, excited as a little kid with a new toy, handed the cell phone toward Robinson, saying, "It's him! It's the President."

Robinson took the phone, and said into it, "Yo, GWB, what's up? I should be mad at your Texas ass, 'cause you are *late* . . . fight's over, tumbleweed blowin' through. You supposed to call when the reporters are watchin', you want it to do either of us some good."

"Kelly, this isn't a social call," the familiar voice said, the usual affability replaced by a new seriousness. "I need to ask you to perform your country a service."

The jokiness was gone now, as Robinson rose and said, "Mr. President, anything."

"It's a matter of national security . . . and international importance."

Robinson's eyes tightened; was this a gag? "Yeah . . ."

"I can't give you any details. All I can say is, you are in a unique position to help America."

Still not quite buying this, wondering if the President and his cabinet buddies had broken out the private stock during the televised fight, and were having fun with the champ, ol' W finally falling off the wagon, Robinson said, "Uh-huh . . . un-huh. . . ."

"It's not a joke, Kelly. Are you willing to be recruited for a mission? Strictly top secret."

"Really?"

"Really."

"Well . . . yeah, man. You got it!"

"Thank you. Kelly, you really *are* a champion. . . . My people with the BNS will be in touch."

"BNS? What's that stand for, sir?"

"That's strictly on a need-to-know basis, Kelly."

"Ah."

"And you don't need to know. . . . Goodbye, Champ."

"Goodbye, Mr. President."

Robinson clicked END and, rather numbly, handed the cell phone back to Darryl. Around him everyone threw questions at him, Darryl pressing with, "Come on, man! What did the head honcho *want*?"

"A favor," Robinson said, feeling shell-shocked. "He says my country needs me."

T.J. snorted a laugh.

Robinson arched an eyebrow and looked at T.J. "What did I just say about your lips and my ass?"

T.J. faded back as Jerry moved forward. "What kind of favor, Kel?"

Now Robinson came out of it, his same cocky self. "He needs me for a top-secret mission."

Another beauty in the entourage called out, "Sweet! Just like double-oh seven!"

"Well," Robinson said, and he flashed the grin. "Maybe a little more like double-oh nine . . . and a half."

But as the party continued, and the beautiful women vied for his attention, Kelly Robinson sat with that grin turning glazed, as he wondered just what his president . . . his country . . . had in store for him.

3

On a bulletin board in the bullpen at BNS headquarters (location undisclosed) was pinned a mock-up of a milk-carton-style missing-child flier. Beneath a caption—HAVE YOU SEEN ME? IF SO, PLEASE CALL 1-888-AIR-FORCE—was a picture of the sleek Switchblade Stealth Fighter/Bomber soaring proudly through a cloud-strewn sky.

Such dry, dark humor was typical of the decent men and women who did dirty jobs for their government, though the bustling bullpen—a warren of desks where agents sat at computers—might have been at an insurance company or engineering firm, rather than the most secret of U.S. spy agencies.

Slightly more casual in his black zippered jacket, blue t-shirt and black slacks than the other agents in their suits and ties, Alexander Scott stepped up to the work area of Chris Kafer, an adroit tech who was assisting him on the Switchblade search. Scott's eye caught USA TODAY folded in half on the tech's desk; a headline said

HERO MOURNED

and a smaller head added

LOST AT SEA WITH HIS JET

Scott picked up the paper and had a better look, and wished he hadn't: the smiling face of Lt. John Percy, a "great American" in the words of the President, gave him a sick feeling. It wasn't so much that Percy didn't deserve the accolade—the traitor obviously didn't, but Scott wasn't one to begrudge a dead guy a little good P.R.

What made him slightly bilious was this prominent, front-page reminder of the mission he had messed up.

Much as he tried to stay positive, telling himself the mission had *mostly* come off just fine, the part where the guy he'd been sent to rescue got killed seemed a noticeable flaw. . . .

Tossing the paper back onto the desk, Scott leaned in over the shoulder of the cherubic tech. "Anything?" Scott asked, noting the satellite photos Kafer was perusing.

Kafer offered a humorless half-smirk. "Kinda tough finding something designed by the best minds in our wonk think-tank to be invisible."

"Just look for any distortions, any irregularities. . . ."

"Alex, these are satellite photos. There are *always* distortions and irregularities."

"Good point. Good point."

Scott patted the tech on the shoulder and headed over to the coffee-break area, where Agent Gary Meyers was standing watching the TV.

The tall, rather beefy agent grinned as he saw Scott approach, and said, "Alex! Check it out. . . ."

Scott joined his colleague and winced as he saw what the agent was watching . . . but then joined him, as—on the screen—a press conference was under way.

The Middleweight Champ, Kelly Robinson, stood behind a Caesar's Palace podium, where multiple microphones picked up his every word of wisdom. The fighter exuded cool self-confidence, even smugness, though he seemed to Scott oddly diminished by the bulk of a black leather flight-type jacket over a yellow hooded sweatshirt adorned with an ostentatious gold necklace and medallion.

"I shouldn't dignify such a dumb-ass question," Robinson was saying. "I'm a professional—you really think I'd prolong a fight till some damn tee-*vee* show was over?"

An off-screen reporter called out: "Certain commentators are saying you gave Lirette a shot 'cause he's a cream-puff—beneath your talent. How do you respond to that, Champ?"

"You take a few shots from Blake, and tell me if you think he's a cream-puff."

Another reporter asked, "Do you think Cedric Mills will give you more of a problem?"

Robinson grinned. "What kinda name is that for a Hungarian? Sounds like where they make breakfast food."

The same reporter followed up: "Mills has something in common with you, Champ—he's never lost a fight."

This seemed to get under Robinson's skin, a little. He jabbed the air with a forefinger as he said, "Let me tell you something, Mr. Hayes. Cedric Mills ain't nothin' but a punk-ass bitch."

Yet another reporter chimed in skeptically: "Come on, Champ—cut the trash talk and give us your real opinion."

The champ flashed his famous grin, so wide it seemed to have an extra half-dozen teeth in it. "My real opinion is you wearin' one butt-ugly tie, Seymour. You dressin' in the dark again?"

The same reporter, chuckling, used to this sort of good-natured abuse from the champ, pressed on. "Kelly, Mills is no Blake Lirette—he's the European Middleweight Champion."

"Of punk-ass bitches." The champ shook his head, and his smile seemed slightly strained now. "See, before the fight, you was saying Blake had a real shot—he was so young and I was so old . . . remember, fellas?"

"Is that why you're taking on two fights in one week, Kelly?" the same reporter asked. "To make a point?"

"Why, don't you fellas wanna work that hard? Have to cover two fights in one week? Look—Kelly Robinson is getting bored. Kelly Robinson needs a *challenge* at this point in his life."

Alexander Scott grabbed the remote and hit MUTE.

"Hey!" the other agent said.

"Guy makes me sick," Scott said.

"What have you got against him? He's the best at what he does. Isn't that what we all strive for?"

Scott made a face, as if he was tasting something unpleasant. "Look at him! Full of himself. Talking about himself in the third-person. Generally I try to keep a good thought, y'know? But that guy . . . he's a pompous, egotistical prick."

"Yeah. Right." And now Agent Meyers made an open handed, finger-curling gesture that meant: *Time to pay up.*

Scott shook his head. "It's not that at all . . ."

"Are you sure you wouldn't like him better, if you didn't keep betting against him?"

With a sigh, Scott dug out his wallet from his back pocket and fished out a fifty, which he handed to Agent Meyers.

"See, I'm betting against him," Scott said, "because I believe a man that self-deluded is bound to fail one day."

"Whatever," Meyers said, placing the fifty in his own billfold.

"Can't help myself. Call it wishful thinking. . . . Double or nothing?"

"On the Mills fight?"

"Yeah."

Meyers dug back in the wallet and handed Scott the bill back, saying, "You're on."

A strikingly attractive blonde, an amazingly well-preserved fifty, appeared at Scott's side as if she'd materialized. Her tawny hair pinned up, her eyes a lively blue behind dark-framed glasses, Edna Penny-weather—utterly professional in a navy blue suit with simple elegant lines—wielded a clipboard the way a warrior carried a shield, though perhaps with slightly more ferocity.

Some agents feared the occasionally icy secretary of McIntyre, the BNS chief; but Scott did not, aware as he was that Miss Pennyweather had an affection for him. Though she knew as well as anyone in the bureau just how many kills the amiable boyish agent had racked up, she clearly found him adorable.

"*There* you are, Alex," she said, crisply. "Mr. McIntyre would like to see you."

They walked and talked together, moving from the bullpen into the adjacent research and development center, a blue-tinged world of cement and steel where gizmos and gadgets—the toys of death and destruction every spy both craved and required—were fashioned by Uncle Sam's own mad scientists.

"So," she said, taking the lead as they headed to the stairway to the walkway above the R & D lab, "how does it feel to be assigned to the agency's biggest case?"

"Well, to be truthful, Edna . . . I'm a little nervous."

"Now, Alex, I'm sure you'll do just fine."

Their shoes pinged off the metal stairs.

"It's not the mission itself," he said, and they were on the walkway now, "it's Rachel. . . . She's been assigned to the mission, too."

"Ah," Miss Pennyweather said, as they clipped along, "you're still carrying the torch, I see."

Scott liked Edna Pennyweather very much—she had often run interference for him with McIntyre; but their relationship was oddly poised between flirtation and a mother-son vibe that seemed to him weirdly incestuous, sometimes. Even though they weren't related or anything. . . .

"Miss Wright is a lovely young woman," Miss Pennyweather was saying. "I can understand why you'd be hung up on her."

He touched her sleeve and they paused next to the railing; below them several massive bright yellow missiles were being tinkered with by BNS minions in white lab coats.

"I'm not 'hung up' on her, Edna . . . okay? I'm not a child."

"Of course you aren't, Alex."

"I'm a trained killing machine." He squinted to demonstrate his cruel nature.

"Of course you are, Alex."

Then they were walking again, heading toward the reception area outside McIntyre's office.

"And trained killing machines don't get hung up on . . ." He sought the right word, and failed. ". . . chicks."

Her mouth twitched in amusement. "Of course they don't, Alex."

"So I'm not hung up on Rachel, or carrying the torch, either. That's not it at all."

"What *is* 'it,' Alex?"

He shrugged, leaned against Miss Pennyweather's desk, which they had reached, and which she was seating herself behind. "I just . . . want to spend some quality time with her. Which is different. Much deeper."

"Unclad quality time, perhaps?"

"Naked would be nice."

Miss Pennyweather peered at him above her glasses. "Relationships at work can be perilous, Alex."

He sighed, widened his eyes. "Tell me about it. But we don't *have* a relationship, Rachel and me . . . so it's not all that dangerous."

While Miss Pennyweather's pretty mouth smiled, her eyes were tight with genuine concern. "Why don't you just . . . tell her?"

"I would . . ."

Miss Pennyweather arched an eyebrow.

"I *will*," Scott corrected. "I mean, we're on the same mission, and. . . . It's just, whenever I try to talk to her on a, you know, social level, I wind up sounding like an idiot."

Footsteps interrupted, and Scott stood straight, turning toward a fellow agent approaching Miss Penny-weather's desk.

A suave tall-dark-handsome thirty-five, Carlos Castillo—in his tailored dark suit, pale blue shirt and dark blue tie—looked as if he'd walked out of the pages of *GQ*. How did the guy manage that snazzy wardrobe on an agent's salary, anyway?

But then Carlos was undoubtedly at the top of the BNS pay scale: the man was legendary within the agency, his success rate with difficult assignments staggeringly high, his case files filled with episodes rivaling anything Ian Fleming or Len Deighton had ever imagined.

Carlos carried a briefcase in one hand and a single red rose in the other—the latter he presented to his boss's secretary, saying in that mellifluous Castilian accent of his, "Good morning, Edna. . . . You are, as always, a vision."

She took the rose with a smile and her eyes and the dashing agent's held for several seconds—long enough for Scott to feel uncomfortable, anyway.

Then, as an afterthought, Carlos noticed Scott, and—with that tiny, ever-so-smug smile that seemed faintly mocking to the younger agent—said, "Alex. You're back from the field, too, I see."

"Hey, Carlos." The hell of it was, despite that questionable smile, the super-agent was invariably a nice guy, where Scott was concerned. "Heard you did an . . . adequate job in Cuba."

"If by 'adequate' you mean I single-handedly averted another Bay of Pigs . . . then yes. And how about you, Alex? How did you fare in the tundra?"

"Oh! Great. Good. You know . . . got the information. Which is the important thing."

Carlos frowned, cocked his head. "What of the pilot? Did you bring him back?"

"Yes. Oh yes. I brought him back. Indeed."

Now Carlos looked genuinely disappointed, albeit in a manner that seemed sympathetic to Scott. "Oh, Alex . . . please tell me you didn't manage to get him killed."

"No! No. I, uh . . . I'd say he got himself killed."

A deep compassionate sigh. "Then you did not effect the rescue."

"Well . . . that depends on how you look at it. Kind of open to interpretation."

"Lt. Percy *is* dead."

"Yeah. A little bit."

The suave agent—he smelled of a musky cologne—slipped an arm around Scott's shoulder. "Listen to me, Alex. Are you listening?"

"Sure."

"Do not let this defeat you. Such results plague even the best of agents."

"Well, I'm a good agent."

"You are an *excellent* agent. And I am proud to serve with you."

With a pat on the back, a wink, and a Sammy Sosa-like two-fingers-to-the-lips farewell kiss, Carlos headed into the adjacent glassed-off room, where returning agents checked in their gear.

"That guy cracks me up," Scott said. "What an ass."

"Yes . . . he has a very nice—"

"I didn't mean it that way!"

The secretary glanced up at him in mild surprise. "I thought you were friends."

"Doesn't he crack you up? I mean, who does he think he is?"

Miss Pennyweather arched an eyebrow. "The agency's pre-eminent agent, perhaps?"

"Well, yeah . . . but he's older than me. Give me time." Scott formed a disgusted smirk in one cheek. "It's like he thinks he's some kind of super-hero or something? Latin Man, maybe . . . or Look-at-me-I'm-so-cool Man."

Miss Pennyweather, ignoring Scott's labored sarcasm, merely said, "He's certainly good-looking enough to be a superhero."

"Really? Good-looking? You think he's good-looking . . . ?"

The secretary viewed Scott with a new twinkle. "Say . . . if Carlos likes to offer you advice, and take you under his wing like that—why not ask *him*?"

"Ask him what?"

"Ask him what approach might work for you, with Miss Wright? Didn't they date for a while?"

"No! No. They absolutely did *not* date. Are you kidding?"

"Well, frankly, Alex, the word around the office is—"

"Edna, please—don't listen to gossip. It's beneath you! Anyway, they just happened to be on stakeout together, for a couple weeks. And, you know—those things just happen. On stakeouts."

"Ah."

"Boredom and stuff. Not any deep feelings or anything."

"I see."

Through the glass wall, Carlos could be seen returning field equipment to a seasoned BNS tech at a counter. Scott couldn't help but notice that all of the gear was top-of-the-line.

"That's a personal escape module," Scott said, astounded. "Do you know what that *goes* for?"

"Not really."

"Well, neither do I, but you just don't send that kind

of high-end deal on some Cuban expedition where it could get. . . . Is that a monofilament cell phone? I thought that was still in development!"

"Perhaps Carlos was field-testing it."

"Mac never trusts me with gear like that." Scott shook his head. "I try to stay positive, Edna, you know?"

"I know."

"But just once I'd like to get sent out into the field with the top-shelf stuff."

"You were assigned a GPS locator, I believe."

"Yes, but have you seen the size of that thing? Edna, that's first-generation technology—clunky and funky. Size does matter, you know."

"Do tell."

"Yes—smaller the better."

She pondered that.

"You see, Edna, in the spy game, the conventional wisdom is reversed. You want people to say, 'Wow, cool—that's so tiny!' 'Man, I can barely *see* that baby!' . . . Not, 'Oh my God, look at the size of your GPS locator!' I mean, do you really think Carlos hears, 'Look at the size of that thing,' very often?"

The secretary, with a private smile, said, "I'll take the fifth on that one, Alex. . . . All I know is, seems everyone in the BNS wants to be like Carlos."

"No," Scott said firmly, pointing a finger, risking being rude. "I do *not* want to be like Carlos. . . . See, he's got seniority, is all. He's older than me. I have the reflexes of youth . . . I don't need gimmicks and gadgets."

"I'm sure you don't." The desk phone buzzed and

Miss Pennyweather lifted the receiver, said, "Yes," listened a while, then said, "I'll send him right in." Hanging up, she gave Scott a reassuring smile and said, "Mac's ready for you."

Scott raised his palms, as if somebody were robbing him. He said to the woman, "You see? Most important mission of the year, and is Mac calling in Carlos? No."

"Better go on in."

"We'll finish this later, Edna. Okay?" He lifted his fingers to his lips, in the Carlos-cum-Sosa style, and said, "Adios."

Scott found McIntyre standing behind his big black modern desk; in his forties, slender but substantial, his hair dark and combed back, his face a narrow oval, his forehead high, Mac might have been an undertaker in that black suit with red-and-black silk tie. The chief of the BNS had an expression of perpetual frustration . . . or at least that was the expression the man always seemed to wear around Alexander Scott.

The lighting in the office was dim, as the wall behind Mac's desk was in view-screen mode, displaying a photograph of a white-haired, rather gnome-ish individual who Scott had never met but nonetheless knew to be Arnold Gundars . . .

. . . the man to whom the late Lt. Percy had claimed to have sold the experimental plane.

Seated across the desk from McIntyre was another man Scott had not met before, but immediately recognized: Army General James Tucker, Joint Chief Chairman. In full uniform, Tucker was a square-jawed, rather grizzled warrior in his mid-fifties.

"General Tucker," McIntyre said, "this is Special Agent Alex Scott."

Scott shook Tucker's hand, said, "General," then took the seat waiting for him. He smiled at the Joint Chief Chairman, just trying to loosen the man up, saying, "I still love hearing that—'Special' Agent. Till just a couple of months ago, I was just a plain ordinary agent . . . y'know, regular, whitebread. Then right around Christmas, I got promoted to Special Agent. That sure was a nice Christmas."

About then Scott realized he was the only one smiling, or for that matter talking, and that in fact the expressions of the other two men were rather glazed.

Scott said, "I mean, under the circumstances, General, that's probably not all that pertinent." Putting on his most business-like face, the special agent said to his boss, "Please, sir . . . continue."

McIntyre said, patiently, "I was just going over the op."

"Great. Fine. I'm there." Scott reached for a pot of coffee on Mac's expansive desk and poured himself a cup as his boss continued the briefing, gesturing from time to time to the looming picture of the gray-haired gnome on the wall screen.

"General, this is Arnold Gundars. Agent Scott here could tell you that Gundars is one of the most successful illegal arms dealers in the world. Our friends at the CIA have access to his overseas accounts, and they tell us that in the past five days, there's been a substantial depletion of funds from those accounts . . . without any reimbursements."

General Tucker sat forward, frowning thoughtfully. "In other words, he's purchased something . . . something big."

"The Switchblade," Mac confirmed.

"But," the general continued, "he hasn't re-sold it . . . yet."

Scott risked another smile at the Joint Chief Chairman. "General, don't worry—I'll get your plane back for you. No problem. Count on it."

Then Scott sipped the coffee, which proved to be scalding. He resisted the urge to spit it out, and scream, doing his best to cover his discomfort, swallowing the boiling liquid.

Nonetheless, the general noticed something wrong with the young agent, and inquired, "Are you all right, son?"

Scott, putting the coffee down, nodded, gave a thumbs up, raised a finger in a "one second" manner, and stepped outside.

Running to the nearest water fountain, glad he had played it so effectively cool, Scott soothed his burning mouth . . .

. . . unaware that the general and McIntyre were watching him through the glass wall.

"You're certain we can't use Castillo?" the general asked McIntyre, while Scott sought relief at the fountain.

"Dead certain, General," McIntyre said. "Last year Carlos infiltrated the biggest arms trading syndicate in Eastern Europe. Short of plastic surgery . . . and we hardly have time for *that* . . . Castillo wouldn't last five minutes on this mission."

"Pity. Damn shame. . . . That Carlos is amazing. Proficient, deadly, an amazing physical specimen all 'round. You know I once happened to open a shower curtain, down in your locker room, and that man is—"

Scott returned, and the conversation was cut off.

"If you don't mind my asking, sir," Scott said to his boss, as he sat back down, "where is Agent Wright? She *is* assigned to this case, isn't she? Shouldn't she be here for the briefing?"

"She's already in Budapest," McIntyre said, "assembling a team, setting up the op center."

"Ah. Good."

"You've worked with Miss Wright before?"

"Oh yes. But this is the first time we'll be on stakeout together. So I'm, you know, kinda looking forward to that."

McIntyre raised an eyebrow. "Actually, this mission doesn't call for a stakeout, Alex."

"Maybe. Maybe not. Let's keep our options open, shall we? Man in the field has to have some leeway."

McIntyre sighed, then he said, "Now the European Middleweight Boxing Championship will be held in Budapest two days from now. Our man Arnold Gundars, as it happens, is a fanatic about the sport of boxing . . . a true aficionado. And he's throwing a sort of pre-match party the night before."

Nodding, Scott said, "Perfect. A classic opportunity for a stakeout."

Rather sharply, Mac said, "Alex, no stakeout." McIntyre handed several stapled sheets of paper across the desk to Scott, then another set to the general. "Now, let's have a look at the guest list. . . ."

Scott perused it quickly. "Wow—this is, like . . . a who's who of global terrorists. Drop a bomb on this party and the world's a happier place, all of a sudden."

"A tempting scenario," Mac admitted, "but our goal is to retrieve the Switchblade . . . and intelligence tells us Gundars is using this party as a cover to sell our plane."

"Remind me," Scott said, as an aside, "I want to talk to you about our intelligence, sometime soon."

"Alex, take a hard look at the aerial photograph of the palace where the party's being held—on the bottom, under the guest list. . . ."

Scott did; then said, "All these major players in the terrorism game, in one place. . . . Security's gonna be tight, Mac."

"We realize that," McIntyre said, "and our best strategists have been going over the situation. They've come up with what I believe is our one chance of getting you inside those walls."

Scott nodded. "Stake the place out, wait for a—"

"No. We've arranged the perfect cover story for you; the ideal cover identity. You'll be accompanying a guest to that party, someone who is already invited."

"You don't mean . . . a *civilian*?"

"Exactly. You'll be working with a civilian to secure entry."

Scott patted the air with his free hand. "Whoa, now, boss. Let's just take a step back, shall we? . . . A civilian's chances of surviving a mission this dangerous are, like, a snowball in—"

"*Special* Agent Scott," the general cut in crisply. His bulldog face was a shade of red tinged with purple. "I don't believe you appreciate the gravity of this situation."

Scott began to reply, but the general kept on going.

"Our best scientific minds," Tucker said, "designed the Switchblade to be an invisible reconnaissance aircraft . . . not just stealth: viable invisibility. Do you know what that would mean?"

This time the agent got his comment in: "It means any person . . . any country . . . could turn the Switchblade into an untraceable system for the delivery of weapons of mass destruction."

The general nodded curtly. "The *only* such untraceable system in existence, Special Agent Scott. Whoever obtains that plane can go anywhere or do anything . . . and no one, no country, would even know who was responsible. That is obviously, utterly, unacceptable. Do I make myself clear?"

"Yes, sir," Scott said.

"And," the general said, settling back in his chair, "if we do have to sacrifice the life of a civilian to get that plane back, well . . . then that's just the price that's going to have to be paid. Clear?"

But Scott said nothing.

His boss knew that the young agent was biting his tongue, and headed off any unpleasantness by dismissing Scott, adding, "I need a few more moments with the general. We'll talk later."

And they did.

Not an hour had gone by when Scott caught up with McIntyre in the hallway, the chief heading briskly to the main conference room.

"Mac," Scott said, working to keep up with his boss, "we don't need a civilian. It's an unnecessary complication—I can find my own way in. It's what I do!"

"Can't risk it, Alex," Mac said, not without affection and even respect for the eager agent. "We don't have enough intelligence to give you a decent leg up on it."

How could Scott argue with that, after the Siberian screw-up?

But nonetheless, Scott pressed on, following McIntyre into the conference room, where several agents sat watching a television monitor on a stand.

"What about the risk of trusting key elements of this mission," Scott said, "to an untrained, most likely incompetent civilian?"

"This is not a matter open for discussion," Mac said tightly.

Now Scott could see what his fellow agents were watching: on the screen was that ubiquitous Kelly Robinson, blathering as usual . . . another press conference, already? Was there no end to the media's interest in this shallow fool?

"We have work to do here," Scott said pointedly, the other agents turning toward him with wide eyes. "Turn that TV off—I'm sick to death of looking at that arrogant asshole's ugly face!"

But the face on the television seemed to be looking at Scott now, and even . . . talking to him. . . .

"You better watch what you say next," Robinson's face on the monitor said intensely, "you frizzy-headed, pale-ass surfer girl."

Scott shook his head, saying to his fellow agents, "Will you listen to that jerk? Bullying the press like that? Tearing into some poor, pathetic reporter—"

"I ain't talkin' to no pathetic reporter," the face on the TV said, eyes wild. "I'm talking to *you*, chump!"

And Scott realized this was not a press session.

With a sideways whisper, he said to Mac, "Uh . . . video conference?"

His boss nodded, smiling faintly. Then he spoke toward the monitor, gesturing to the agent. "Alex Scott—meet Kelly Robinson. You two will be working together on this mission."

Whispering, Scott said, "*This* is my civilian?"

Sotto voce, Mac responded: "That is your civilian."

With an embarrassed smile, Scott shambled forward toward the monitor, where his eyes met the boxer's. "Hey—what can I say? . . . Big fan."

4

··

At a private gate at McCarran International Airport in
Las Vegas, a sleek white-topped blue-bellied Gulf-
stream private jet—emblazoned with the flourish of a
red-outlined-yellow logo/signature: KELLY ROBIN-
SON—awaited its namesake. The jet had a lovely afternoon to fly into . . . the sky an eggshell blue, the
clouds snow-white and wispy, half-hearted, the sun
hot but not out of hand . . . if, of course, the Middleweight Champion of the World ever deigned to be-
stow his presence.

Takeoff time had been scheduled for three P.M., but
the gleaming white super-stretch Lincoln Navigator
SUV-limo—hip-hop blasting from its open sun-
roofs—did not roll onto the tarmac to a stop until well
after four. Back doors swung open and the champ's
posse—burly bald Jerry, slender bald Darryl, wiry
T.J., to a man decked out in purple and black KELLY
ROBINSON running suits—stepped out, stretching,
reacting to the bright sunlight as if they'd been in a
cave all day. They were followed by a quartet of
shapely young women—one white, two black, one
Asian, in low tops and bare midriffs and tight slacks—

whose high sprayed hair and heavy make-up could not defeat their natural beauty.

Finally, all in black—from his narrow-brimmed hat and sunglasses to his untucked turtleneck and slightly baggy trousers (though a silver medallion did wink at the sun, the sun winking back)—Kelly Robinson emerged, waving a heavily jeweled hand like a benevolent potentate.

Speaking to the young women, he said, "Ladies, last night was very special . . . I believe we struck a blow for world peace and racial harmony."

They beamed at him, each feeling "very special."

"So personal, so intimate," he said softly, earnestly. He tapped his heart with two fingers. "I mean that. . . . And that goes out to all four of y'all."

Each flashed him a personal, intimate smile, as the young women piled back into the limo.

Robinson turned, business-like, to his crew. "All right, fellas—let's do it."

And as his posse unloaded the SUV, and dealt with the bags, Kelly Robinson headed into the airport, to the nearby VIP lounge, not noticing the unprepossessing blond secret agent in the green corduroy jacket and brown slacks who tagged after him.

Though he took his president's call to arms quite seriously, Robinson had the upcoming fight on his mind; his agreement to aid his country, by helping some government operative slip into a party, seemed no biggie. The fight, two days from now, was the thing.

And he felt good, considering not forty-eight hours had passed since he traded blows with Blake Lirette (*not* a cream-puff), though he knew going straight into another championship fight had its risks.

At thirty-six, he was old for the fight game; he had no intention of being some damn George Foreman— he planned to retire undefeated, a year from now . . . or maybe two. He couldn't see himself fighting past forty.

The problem was, though, Kelly Robinson couldn't see himself *not* fighting. . . . This was who he was, a modern gladiator; this was what he had trained to be since a damn impoverished childhood, working his way up through neighborhood Golden Gloves tourneys to the Olympics itself.

For all his confidence—and it was no pose: this man believed in himself—Kelly Robinson was human. In quiet moments, within himself, he had doubts. Not in his ability, no—but in his future. What would he be, who would he be, after the final bell rang on his fight career?

Robinson sat at the VIP table, with a view on the tarmac and his private jet, where Jerry and the rest of his posse were still unloading the SUV. The champ wanted to grab a bite on the ground, before heading to the other side of the planet.

"Hey," someone said.

Robinson looked up.

For a moment, the champ didn't recognize the secret agent: the man, after all, was fairly ordinary-looking, a slender, pleasant guy distinguished only by a misshapen, frequently broken nose and blond bangs. Robinson didn't remember the man's name.

"I'm Alex Scott," the guy said, smiling embarrass-
edly. "We met yesterday . . . sort of. On TV?"

"Yeah," Robinson said. "You the 'big fan' who
hates my ugly asshole face."

Scott winced, sitting next to Robinson. "Yeah . . .
that was tactless. I'm really sorry about that."

Robinson just looked at him.

Scott fumbled on: "See, I had a job go a little
wrong, the other day, been under a lot of stress at
work, kind of thing. . . ."

The champ glared at him. "Do I look like Oprah? I
ain't your damn wife. . . . Keep your problems to
yourself."

This encounter had been witnessed, through the
window, by the burly Jerry, who had summoned the
champ's retinue, and now the formidable trio of Jerry,
T.J. and Darryl were piling into the VIP area.

Scott glanced up to find himself flanked by Robinson's posse; the massive Jerry, like a traffic cop, held
up a palm no bigger than a trash-can lid.

"Just step away from the man," Jerry said menacingly.
"Champ ain't givin' out no autographs, s'afternoon."

"Jerry, I appreciate the good thought," Robinson
said. "But this is Alex, the new personal assistant I told
you I was takin' on."

T.J. stepped forward, frowning. "What about me? I
thought I was your 'personal' assistant! What kinda
lame-ass shit—"

Now it was Robinson who held up a traffic-cop
palm. "T.J.—this is my other assistant. My *new* assistant . . . phone call from the Prez, remember?"

T.J. brightened. "Oh yeah! The secret mission."

Alex Scott leaned on an elbow and covered his face.

T.J. turned to Jerry, as he gestured toward Scott. "He's the mission man."

Jerry nodded, eyes tightening. "Right. The, uh . . . challenged one."

Scott looked up, curiously.

"No offense," Jerry said.

"None taken," Scott said, but it came out almost a question.

T.J. leaned in, grinning, jerking a thumb out the window, toward the pile of bags. "There you go, Mr. New Personal Assistant. Those go on the jet."

Then the trio sauntered outside.

The secret agent was clearly pissed, saying under his breath, "You *told* them about the mission?"

"They don't know shit about the mission. They were just there when GWB called."

"GWB. . . . So what do they think the mission *is*? Who do they think I *am*?"

Robinson smiled, shaking his head. "You gotta learn to chill, son. Relax. Told 'em my 'secret mission' is givin' the President's backward nephew a job."

Scott blinked. "I'm sorry . . . what?"

"I tol' 'em you're mentally challenged."

"Retarded."

"Yeah—but you'll be glad to know you did jus' fine in the Special Olympics last year. Drool a little, if you get a chance; maybe we'll put a bike helmet on you, case you bang into walls and shit."

"You think this is funny?"

"Lighten up, Scotty. That was somethin' I told my boys to give you a . . . what do you spy guys call it? A cover story."

Scott's eyes tightened. "A cover story. I already have a cover story—I'm your new personal assistant."

"Yeah, well, I just put my own spin on it . . . so it would sit better with my crew. You see, you're in *my* world now, Scotty."

"It's Scott, or Alex."

"Call me Kelly. I don't stand on ceremony."

"Well, the BNS does. You don't seem to understand what sort of situation you and I are about to find ourselves in."

A waitress came over, and Robinson ordered coffee, black, and Scott didn't want anything.

Then Robinson asked, "What does BNS stand for, anyway? I mean, I never even heard of it."

"You're not supposed to have heard of it."

"Aw come on . . . we're workin' together now, right, Scotty? What's BNS stand for?"

"If I told you, I'd have to kill you."

Robinson howled with laughter. "You could try! I'll tell you what it stands for: the Bullshit Never Stops."

Scott was shaking his head. "I think you got the wrong idea about how this relationship is going to work."

"Relationship? Do I?"

"You're acting like you're the Harlem Globetrotters and I'm those . . . *white* guys who are just sent out to lose and look like idiots."

"I'm glad we're getting our 'relationship' defined, early and shit."

"Kelly—that is not how it's going to go." The blond agent leaned in, his blue eyes strangely hard. "*I* am Meadowlark Lemon."

"You're Meadowlark Lemon."

"Understand? Play your cards right, and maybe . . . just maybe . . . I'll let you be my Curly Neil."

"Okay, Meadowlark. Cool with that." The champ wagged a head toward the window, through which the pile of luggage could be seen, waiting. "Now get my bags loaded on the damn plane."

And Kelly Robinson got up, took a paper cup of coffee from the approaching waitress ("My assistant will get the check") and headed out onto the tarmac, where his boys were milling, and went up onto his jet.

When a frustrated Alex Scott exited the airport onto the tarmac, he noticed skinny T.J. pacing around, talking into a cell phone, clearly having problems.

"No, I'm *not* Kelly Robinson," T.J. was saying. "Kelly Robinson don't make his own phone calls."

Scott believed that. He'd been at McCarran since noon, having been told they'd take off at three P.M. and wanting plenty of time to check out the security situation. About three-thirty, Scott had noticed the private jet's low-key African-American pilot sitting in the VIP area, reading the Las Vegas *Sun*.

"I thought we were leaving at three," Scott had said to the pilot, who—without even looking up—had advised the agent to stop going by Pacific Standard Time and set his watch to Kelly Robinson Time. Which the pilot further defined as throwing your damn watch away.

"I'm trying to confirm the man's reservations," T.J. was saying into the cell. "What's the matter with you? Speak English!"

The burly bearded guy, the one called Jerry, approached the perplexed T.J., who looked up to ask, "What the hell does '*cia, seqit, hedlek, hodj*' mean, anyway?"

Jerry said, "It means, sure I speak English, sucker—just not to you."

Wind riffling his wheat-color hair, Scott ambled over. "You want some help?"

T.J. frowned. "Aren't you supposed to be gettin' those bags?"

"It's just . . ." Scott held out his hand, palm up. ". . . I speak a little Hungarian."

Jerry and T.J. stared at him, skeptically; then T.J. shrugged, handed the phone forward, saying, "What the hell, man—knock yourself out."

Scott quickly realized he was talking to a desk clerk at a hotel in Budapest; speaking fluent Hungarian, the agent soon had a grasp of the situation.

"*Pince, barak, olcson,*" Scott said. "*Kusenum. . . .*" He turned toward the amazed pair of the champ's assistants, and gave them the high sign. Then, still in Hungarian, he told the clerk over the crackly line, "Mr. Robinson would like a basement room . . . barracks-style, if possible."

The desk clerk said (in Hungarian, of course), "Oh,

but sir . . . Mr. Robinson is a great champion, and a celebrity. Surely he would like the penthouse."

"No, Mr. Robinson is a real eccentric—his idea of training is to deprive himself. He would prefer his personal assistant, Alexander Scott, be booked into the duplex penthouse."

"Whatever you say, sir."

With a smile, Scott handed the phone back to T.J. "Okay, guys—everything is set."

"All right," T.J. said. "Okay . . ."

Scott said, "Since I did you a favor, how about you get those bags for me?"

And, without waiting for an answer, Alexander Scott headed up and onto the plane.

He did not see the two men exchange puzzled glances, nor did he hear Jerry say to T.J., "Better watch your ass, man—that Special Olympics clown's got skills. He'll have your job."

About an hour later, as the jet streaked into a sky made purple and orange by the sunset, toward the rear of the sumptuous private plane, Alexander Scott was bonding with his fellow Kelly Robinson assistant T.J., as the two men sat at a double-monitor set-up, playing "BLOOD WARRIOR 6: Dawn of the Defiled" on Playstation 2.

Right now, on T.J.'s monitor, a video warrior was wandering through a dark, spooky, vault-like chamber. T.J.'s guy unleashed a barrage of automatic gunfire, as well as several concussion grenades, decimating a wall . . . but revealing no sign of Scott's man.

"Huh," T.J. said to himself, more than his fellow gamer at the monitor and controls beside him, "where you at, man?"

T.J. swiveled his guy around . . . and then Scott's man was standing right there, right behind him, with a huge pistol aimed at the video warrior's skull.

"Uh oh," T.J. said, and his fingers flew . . .

. . . but not fast enough: Scott triggered his warrior's weapon, and T.J.'s guy got his head blown clean off, with spurting gore to make the obvious point.

Lunch Box, a heavy-set member of the Robinson posse whose name was all too accurate, leaned in at T.J.'s station and said, "Damn, man! Retard just blew your damn *head* off!"

T.J. gave Scott a long, slow, suspicious glare. Then he said, "Special Olympics my ass."

They did not begin another game, however, because the burly Jerry came trundling to the rear of the plane, saying, "Shit! . . . Champ's at it again!"

The seat belt sign had just flashed on.

Scott looked around, in confusion, as the posse was finding seats and buckling up, to the tune of assorted coarse exclamations—"Oh man!" "Oh shit!" "Maaan, whathehell!"

Scott rose from the video-game console, asking Jerry, who was buckled in now, "So, Robinson's done with his phone interview?"

"What phone interview?"

"He told me I couldn't . . ." Scott almost said "brief" but substituted as best he could. ". . . talk to him, 'cause he had an important phone interview."

"Hell no. Man was nappin'. . . . But he's up now!"

Not understanding these expressions of concern, Scott moved quickly, irritatedly, forward. In Robinson's private compartment adjacent to the cockpit, Scott was surprised to find Robinson absent, though his face—on magazine covers, scattered around the plush digs—was omnipresent. The co-pilot was sitting on a sofa, reading one of those magazines, *People* from a few months ago. The man glanced up at Scott, then returned to his reading.

Scott tried the cockpit door, found it unlocked, and within were Robinson—sitting calmly at the controls—and the pilot, arms folded, looking on protectively.

"Kelly," Scott said, over the engine throb, "we need to talk."

Robinson said nothing, his eyes flicking from the controls to the orange-streaked sky stretching out before him like a vividly rendered abstract painting, God working in bold brushstrokes.

"I need to fill you in," Scott said firmly. "Kelly!"

No reaction.

"We're on a tight schedule, and you have to be briefed."

"I never wear briefs," Robinson said lightly.

"We're landing at six, and need to be at the palace, at Gundars's party, by eight. Before then, we have a lot to go over."

Robinson glanced back at the intruder. "Somethin' wrong with your eyesight? Didn't you see me turn on the seat-belt sign?"

And the champ pulled the stick back hard, sending the plane into a sudden, steep climb . . .

. . . and launching Alexander Scott, tumbling backward down the center aisle of the plane, through the champ's luxurious cabin, knocking open the door, and spilling past the posse, buckled in their seats. The champ's retinue watched the agent's plunge dispassionately, perhaps having anticipated as much.

Then the plane leveled out, and Scott regained his footing. As he passed the posse on his way back to the cockpit, Scott noted their smirks and chuckles, and said to them, "Your boss is hilarious. Funny guy. Fun-*knee*. Barrel of laughs. . . ."

When Scott got back to the forward section of the plane, Robinson was exiting the cockpit, and the co-pilot was slipping back in.

Scott approached the champ, but Robinson moved past him, heading toward a comfy first-class-style seat, saying, "Let me tell you something, James Blond. . . . This 'mission' ain't gonna operate on your schedule. You are taggin' with me, and I am not taggin' with you, you dig?"

Coming around and blocking the champ from his seat, Scott said, "You are my cover . . . my way into the party. But the mission has its own schedule. And you have to honor it, or both our asses'll be hanging out."

"Well, your white one'll make a better target." Robinson shook his head, grinning. "Scotty, listen to the champ: Kelly Robinson ain't never showed up at a party at eight oh-damn-clock! Not in his life, and he ain't gonna start now."

Now it was Scott's turn to shake his head. "Do you plan to refer to yourself in the third-person all of the time? 'Cause I don't know if I can handle that. Gonna get irritating."

"Well, you won't be irritated till eleven o'clock, will you? 'Cause that's when I'm gonna show up at the festivities."

Robinson started to slip by the agent, who touched his arm . . . gently. "Kelly, we can't risk that. Man, the party could be cleared out by eleven."

"What the hell kinda lame-ass party clears out by eleven? Look, if they are clearin' out, when my smiling face shows up, they will change their damn minds and turn around. Kelly Robinson has *got* to be fashionably late, you dig?"

Scott heaved a sigh. "Kelly—this King of the Universe bull has got to stop. It's fine for your ring persona . . ."

"My what?"

". . . but this isn't a game. This is life and death, not just for us, but for people all over the world. And with an attitude like that, you can bring down the entire mission."

Robinson considered that for a moment, but then his ego kicked back in, and he said, "Let me tell you, Brian Wilson, just what will 'bring down' a mission— a lame-ass party that clears out at eleven."

Scott pawed the air, half-turned away. "You know what? Forget it."

"I will. You're not thinkin' it through, man—Kelly Robinson shows up on time, this Gundars guy will be suspicious. *What's up with that?* he'll say. And the mission'll be deader than disco."

"Tell you what, Kelly—don't worry yourself. Darryl'll get me in—or T.J."

Robinson horse-laughed. "Oh yeah, that's a good plan. That'll work."

Scott looked at his wristwatch, but he wasn't checking for the time; with the thumb and middle finger of his right hand, he popped open the watch case, and revealed two small clear discs in a hidden compartment.

"I just hope," Scott said, glancing toward the rear of the plane, "that the optical diaphanous polyalloy transducers fit one of *their* retinas. . . . These were especially designed for yours."

And the secret agent shut the watch case and began to slip around the champ, saying, "Excuse me."

Now it was Robinson who stopped Scott with a hand on the arm, not so gently. "Whoa whoa whoa! . . . What was that in your watch?"

Scott shrugged, seemingly calm; the truth was, he was excited about the devices: for once he had been entrusted with top-shelf toys, of a sort usually reserved for Carlos Castillo himself.

The agent said, casually, "It's part of the mission, is all. . . . Kinda cool, actually. See, you . . . that is, T.J. . . . will wear this . . ." He popped the watch back open. ". . . and I will wear this."

"Contact lenses?"

"Sorta. Only we'll each wear only one lens. One is the sender, the other the monitor. I wear the sender, and the one wearing the monitor can see everything *I* see . . . out of one eye. Takes some getting used to . . . seeing two things at once . . . but I'm sure T.J. is up to it. Guy seems pretty sharp. . . . Excuse me."

"Hold up," the champ said, frowning. "I don't want T.J. gettin' his nasty, disgusting eye-juice all over *my* polyalloy diaphragm thingie. . . . Give it up."

Scott shrugged, and carefully handed the monitor lens to Robinson, who held it up to the light, having a close look. In the meantime, Scott pushed a small blue button on the side of his watch, positioning the sending "camera" lens to broadcast the Alex Scott view of the world.

"Let's do it," Scott said, and leaned forward, lens on a fingertip, and inserted the sending lens.

Robinson, his imagination seized, did the same with the monitor lens.

The two men faced each other, and Scott couldn't keep from being amused and even charmed, a little, by the champ's child-like glee at seeing himself through Scott's shared "eye." Robinson posed for himself, preened, admiring his own beauty; then, clearly blown away, he shook his head, laughing.

"Yes, Scotty," he said, "we are definitely gonna use these bad boys at the par-tay . . ."

"All right."

". . . at eleven."

Scott frowned. "Kelly, these aren't toys—they allow us to—"

Robinson held up a hand. "Meeting over. Kelly Robinson said eleven, and eleven it is."

The champ sat down, selected a magazine—*US*—

with his picture on it, and began to read, with some pleasure, the article about himself, obviously trying to get used to seeing two images simultaneously, and ignoring one.

The secret agent thought for a moment, then turned toward the cockpit.

"Where you off to?" Robinson asked, perhaps distracted by the movement in the monitor lens.

Scott said nothing, opening the cockpit door and stepping inside, thinking, *Kelly Robinson is about to change his mind . . . and maybe even his tune. . . .*

The two pilots were at the controls, and Scott smiled and nodded to them, and they did likewise back.

"What's our altitude, fellas?" the spy asked.

One pilot said, "Thirty-six five."

"Good to know," Scott said, reaching under his corduroy jacket, "good to know."

He fired the tranq gun first at the pilot, then at the co-pilot, and the two men slumped at the controls, darts in their necks.

Kelly Robinson was already out of his seat, having seen all this through the monitor lens, and was rushing toward the cockpit, fighting the g-force, yelling, "What the hell! What the hell are you *doing,* man?"

By the time the champ stumbled into the cockpit, the jet was in a steep descent.

Standing behind the two slumped-over pilots, bracing himself on the bulkhead, Scott said off-handedly, "Kelly—didn't you see me turn the seatbelt sign on?"

The jet was losing altitude quickly, and Robinson

was freaking out. "What did you do to the pilots, man? You didn't *kill* 'em, did you? You *crazy*? We gonna *crash*!"

Scott blinked. "Wait a second . . . I thought *you* could fly the plane."

"I can't fly no damn plane! They just put it in auto-pilot, and let me hold the stick. Sometimes they let me do a little shit, but . . . damn, it's what *all* the celebrities do!"

"Interesting," Scott said. "That's something I didn't know."

"Don't you read *People*?"

"No. More a *Newsweek* guy . . . *Rolling Stone,* sometimes, if I like the cover story . . ."

"We're gonna damn *die*!"

The plane was nosing toward the earth, so this seemed a reasonable observation.

Scott said, "I save your ass, you go to the party at eight? With me. Deal?"

"Deal! Done deal, whatever—just do something."

The agent stepped forward, shifted the pilot out of his seat and jumped in, taking the controls, pulling the plane out of its nose dive, righting it within seconds.

"Kelly Robinson," Kelly Robinson said, "has been played."

"A little bit," Scott said, cool, confident at the controls.

"You're a pilot. . . . You were messing with my ass, this whole time."

"Little bit."

Robinson leaned forward, and popped the contact

lens into his palm, and tossed it toward Scott, who caught it.

"See you at eleven," Robinson said.

And the champ was gone.

Alexander Scott, flying the plane, shook his head. He realized those tranq darts wouldn't wear off for several hours, meaning he would have neither the opportunity to brief Robinson further, nor to grab a few winks to rest up for the long night ahead. He would be busy flying Kelly Robinson's private jet.

This would have never happened to Carlos, he thought.

5

....

Straddling the banks of the Danube, Budapest had risen again and again from the ashes of warfare, from the eleventh-century Mongols to the twentieth-century Soviets, and as such this bustling cultural and industrial center seemed the perfect setting for a modern clash of east and west—a championship prizefight. Let the venerated city, at the crossroads of Central Europe, play host to a more or less friendly battle, for a change.

Kelly Robinson had never been to Hungary before, and—like many tourists from the west—was astounded by the mix of the cosmopolitan and the archaic represented by Budapest, this city of great Old World allure and welcome modern conveniences.

At the airport, for example—and Robinson was unsure just how much of this was a hospitable attitude toward foreigners, or maybe Presidential (even BNS) influence—he and his posse had been whisked through with a minimum of bureaucratic b.s. A pair of limos had ushered them into a fairytale realm of cobblestone streets and quaint courtyards, where painstakingly maintained Gothic, Baroque and Renaissance homes sprouted like living postcards.

On the same route, however, the thriving city's post-Communist restaurants and cafes, markets and craft fairs, and bars and go-go clubs, indicated a world where Kelly Robinson and his streetwise retinue would have no trouble fitting in.

In the limo, T.J. had reminded Robinson that this part of the globe wasn't ideal for a boxer in training.

"You got to stay away from the goulash, Kel," T.J. told him; the assistant had done his homework. "And the dumplings and the rich desserts. . . . Suckers cook *everything* in lard, over here!"

"Well thank you, Duncan the hell Hines," Robinson said to his sometimes too-helpful aide-de-camp. "The fight's tomorrow. I think I can lay off the strudels till then."

"Strudels of *all* kinds!" T.J. said, raising a forefinger, lecture-style. "You don't want your manly fluids drained, night before the fight!"

Robinson arched an eyebrow at his assistant. "My manly fluids is my business . . . you dig?"

"Sure, Kel. You got it, Kel."

Mother hens. Ever since he took up this sport, when his own mama was still around to look after him, Kelly Robinson had been plagued by well-meaning mother hens, damn 'em all.

Bless them.

The spires of the city were piercing the night by the time the two limos—Robinson had made sure the BNS agent rode in the other one—arrived at the Mercure Hotel Budapest Nemzeti. The Baroque facade appealed to Robinson—the baby-blue coloration and all

that gingerbread spelled out quaintness, and class. Yet
they were located in a busy central area in the Pest part
of Budapest, which looked to have no shortage of
lively nightlife.

The hotel lobby—high-ceilinged, elaborate, with
arches and pillars and wrought-iron rails—was vast
and sumptuous. For one who'd risen from humble beginnings to the championship of the world, Robinson
relished the perks of celebrity, savored his ability not
only to enter such rarefied levels of society all over the
map, but to be invited by hosts everywhere to do so
with eagerness and admiration.

"T.J.," Robinson said, sliding an arm around his
slender second, as they ambled to a check-in counter
smaller than the *Titanic,* "you did all right. You did
just fine."

Ten minutes later, in the tiny, dingy basement room—
with furniture that had apparently been bequeathed to
the hotel from the set designer of Hungarian television's
version of the *Honeymooners*—Kelly Robinson, his
eyes wide and wild, faced his cowering assistant.

"T.J., you blew it. You blew it bigtime!"

T.J. was patting the air. "It wasn't my fault. It was
the white boy's fault."

The rest of the posse was crowded into the glorified
closet, bumping into each other, jammed around the
ancient iron bed, dislodging faded framed prints of the
Danube. The place was strictly from Hungary.

"Oh really?" Robinson asked.

"Yeah! It was him on the phone; he booked it—he
speaks their jibber-jabber. *He's* your new assistant."

"Right. I forgot . . . my bad."

T.J. smiled generously. "No, boss—it ain't your fault. You ain't to blame at all."

Robinson's nostrils flared like those of a stallion about to buck some poor bastard. "Remind me—who is it gets *paid* for bein' my assistant?"

T.J. frowned a little. "That be . . . me."

"And who did I put in charge of gettin' me a hotel room in this fine old city?"

"Uh . . . that be me, again."

"So . . . who was it I should blame?"

With a wide, who-the-hell-else open-armed shrug, T.J. said, "The *white* boy!"

Robinson breathed in and out, slowly; he did not want to waste his energy on this bullshit. He had a fight in twenty-four hours.

So he calmly said, "I'm going back downstairs . . ."

Raising a correcting finger, T.J. said, "Boss, there's no downstairs downer than these downstairs."

Robinson flashed the blinding grin and all around him winced. ". . . I'm sorry. I forgot: we're *in* the basement. Why don't I go *upstairs,* then?"

T.J.'s grin was not blinding. "Good idea."

Robinson beamed at his assistant, placed a hand on the smaller man's shoulder, as if the boxer were speaking to a wayward son. "And you have five minutes to get my ass into the nicest, most expensive, most extravagant suite in this hotel. Or else face the consequences."

"Consequences?" T.J. said, alarmed. "What kind of consequences, Kel?"

"I don't even know yet," Robinson admitted. "I can't think underground . . . but it's gonna be some nasty-ass shit."

T.J. squinted, obviously not relishing this possibility. "I'm on it, Kel—all over the sucker."

"Good. Otherwise you might find out there *is* a downstairs downer than this."

A few minutes later, in a brown leather jacket and darker brown slacks, Robinson—having tried unsuccessfully to call Alex Scott's suite—strode out the front of the hotel, to grab a bite to eat . . . by himself. Hell with those fools. . . .

He almost tripped over Scott, who was seated on the steps, off to one side. The secret agent looked a tad haggard—perhaps from having to fly the jet all that way—but had freshened up some, wearing a brown corduroy jacket over a black shirt with brown slacks.

Robinson noted this color coordination, between him and the agent, and it irritated him, somehow. He resented being connected in any way to this intrusive son of a bitch.

"How's your room?" Scott asked, conversationally.

Robinson just looked down at him.

Scott's shrug was tiny. "I have a beautiful suite . . . probably the nicest in the hotel. I hope you got a room facing the inner courtyard, 'cause the rooms on the street here can be a little loud. And I know you need your rest . . . big fight coming up and all."

"Did I say we'd hit that party at eleven? I should revise that."

Scott smiled, just a little. "Good."

"Make it midnight."

The agent rose and faced the boxer. "You know, Kelly, we could stop sparring, and work together . . . be a lot easier."

"I ain't a team sport player, or maybe you didn't notice."

"Why don't we get a bite, just the two of us? Discuss it?"

Robinson laughed humorlessly. "Yeah, you can be my translator and shit."

"Glad to . . . but you won't need me for that. Hungarians are famous for their hospitality—love talking to westerners. A lot of 'em know English."

But Robinson was only half-heartedly listening, as a strikingly beautiful black-haired woman—slim but shapely in a mini-length black-leather coat with matching black boots—strolled by, her eyes widening at the sight of the famous fighter.

The beauty paused, asking, "Excuse me . . . I don't mean to be rude. . . ."

Robinson smiled; that gypsy-type accent was sexy as hell, not that this doll needed any help.

She was saying, "You . . . could you be . . . Kelly Robinson?"

Robinson shrugged. "Who's Kelly Robinson?"

Her eyes narrowed as she shook her head, arcs of dark hair brushing her shoulders. "Oh, he's a very famous boxer. . . . He's coming to town, and I thought—"

"You thought right, baby."

Her eyes saucered and her smile was glorious. "I can't believe it! Can I be so lucky?"

Robinson moved closer to her. "This could be your lucky night."

She was gushing, now: "I know you from the advertisements for your scent . . . your . . . how is it you say, perfume?"

"It ain't perfume, honey—it's cologne."

"Yes, yes! 'Kelly Robinson wears it—you should, too. . . . It'll knock her out—TKO!' "

He chuckled. "That's right. This must be quite a thrill for you."

"Oh yes, tell me . . . do you really wear this scent?"

"Why don't *you* tell *me*?"

She leaned in and breathed in deeply; nearby, Scott was taking all of this in, right now rolling his eyes.

"My knees," she said, "they are weak."

"That's one of the usual symptoms."

She pressed her hands together and held them to her bosom. "Please—I would love to go to your room, and get your autograph."

"I could give you an autograph right here . . ."

Now her smile turned naughty. "But the kind of personal autograph I would like is . . . better written with some thought and, uh, care . . . and best done in private."

Suddenly Scott stepped forward, and took Robinson's arm. "Kelly—moment of your time?"

Robinson frowned at Scott, then smiled at the beauty, saying, "Hold that thought, baby. . . . *What?*"

Scott whispered, "Careful, man—the hotel's nice, but we are close to a seedy part of town. She could be a thief or drug dealer or streetwalker. . . ."

"Get out of here!" He pulled away from the agent,

and was pleased to find the beauty in black leather still
standing there, displaying that stunning smile, not to
mention those lovely legs. . . .

"Now," Robinson said, "you wanted an autograph."

She moved very close to him, touching his chest
with one hand, her other sliding down his thigh. "Very
much. . . ."

"I heard that," he said. Then he glared over at Scott.
"Only my hotel room ain't ready!"

She shrugged. "Then let's go to mine . . . it's just
across the street."

And she slipped her arms around his neck and
kissed him on the mouth—passionately, her tongue
flicking.

"Baby," Robinson said, when he came up for air,
"lead the way."

She took his hand and began to lead him off; but
Scott grabbed Robinson by the arm again, more force-
fully this time, pulling the man aside. The woman,
hands on hips, glared at Scott, openly annoyed.

Whispering harshly, Scott said to Robinson, "Just
what the hell do you think you're doing?"

"If you don't know, you need to get out more."
Robinson yanked his arm free. "Anyway, I ain't doin'
nothin' yet . . . but in about five minutes—"

"Kelly, please listen to me . . . carefully." He spoke
very softly but intensely. "You are for all intents and
purposes a spy now . . . in hostile territory."

"Spies I seen in movies do just what I'm going to."

"Spies in movies can afford to go walking off with
a strange woman in a strange city . . . you can't."

Robinson shook his head, grinned at the agent con-descendingly. "I'm Kelly Robinson—fifty-seven and oh. Walking off with strange women is one of my fa-vorite hobbies. . . . Live with it."

And Robinson took the beauty's hand and took off down the sidewalk. He did not hear Alexander Scott, behind him, mimicking: "Walking off with strange women. . . ."

The heels on the young woman's boots clicked as the two strolled around the corner, down a darker street than the previous main drag. Robinson felt un-easy, suddenly, but shrugged it off; he would not let that damn secret agent get to him. . . . Why should the middleweight champion of the world be afraid of a young woman?

"I live a block over," she said, and she gestured to an alleyway. "Quicker this way. . . ."

He eased an arm around her shoulder as they headed down the dark, narrow alley, its cobblestones damp and glistening, catching stray light. The sound of a vehicle turning into the alley signaled Robinson to make room, and, without looking, he eased himself and his companion to one side.

But the vehicle—a dark van—screamed past, way the hell faster than it could have any good reason to, and damn near sideswiped Robinson.

"Yo, asshole!" he yelled. "Watch where you're goin'! Damn—there's a *lady* here!"

At that, the van screeched to a stop.

Robinson, startled, backed up a little, arm slipping away from the beauty.

He guessed Scott was right: lot of 'em *did* speak English here. . . .

And now, men started to pile out of the van—four of them, also in black leather jackets, husky suckers, too . . . and then they were right there, all around him, thrusting automatic weapons at him.

He was just thinking, *Damn, that's some bad road rage right there,* when one of the assailants yanked something down over the champ's head—a burlap bag!—and hands were on him, felt like a dozen mitts grabbing, clutching, and he struggled but was badly outnumbered, then he was tossed, hard. He felt himself hit metal, and realized he'd been thrown into the back of the van.

The engine roared to life and tires squealed, confirming his theory. *Least they hadn't harmed the girl,* he thought.

Robinson didn't say anything—he kept his cool. He knew the threat of kidnapping was something that faced every celebrity; and he also knew these were somebody's goons. As a man who himself travelled with his own crew, Robinson figured these clowns were not worth yakking at—he would talk to their leader, reason with him, charm him, buy Kelly Robinson's way out of this shit. . . .

But in less than ten minutes, the bag yanked off his head, Kelly Robinson found himself bound to a chair in a small corner warehouse room, the lighting dim, the goons all around him with weapons thrusting.

Oddly, the voice that spoke from the darkness was

female: "How long have you been working for the United States government?"

"Kelly Robinson don't work for nobody but Kelly Robinson."

The owner of the voice stepped into the light, moving close to him: *the beauty in black leather!*

So the leader was a *she* . . . and that damn Scotty had been right from the jump. . . .

"How long have you been an American agent?" she demanded, her eyes cold and probing, that accent seeming not near so fetching now. She was as lovely as ever, but he no longer felt the least bit attracted to her.

"I don't work for no government, baby—I work for the United States of Kelly Robinson."

One of the goons—pockmarked, pale, his hair dark and thick—leaned in and pressed the snout of an automatic weapon to the fighter's throat.

The goon said, "On your plane, your private jet, there was a BNS agent."

"I don't know what you're talkin' about. What is that, a cable channel? All night news?"

"Who was this man? His name?"

"Listen, all that paprika ain't doin' wonders for your breath . . . so you might back off a bit."

The gun snout pressed harder. "His *name*!"

"You watchin' too many spy movies; I got a news flash for you, fellas and girl—that Austin Powers flick, it wasn't a documentary."

The beauty said, "Cut off his penis."

Flashing that famous grin to the quartet of goons,

Robinson said, "Did I say I didn't know who that fella was? What I meant to say was, I'll be happy to answer whatever questions you gentlemen . . . and lady . . . might have."

The beauty held out her hand, palm up; one of her men filled that gentle palm with a knife—six gleaming inches of steel, two inches wide tapering to a deadly point.

"Who," she asked, "is this agent?"

"Well, he's blond," Robinson said, with quick insincere affability. "I don't know if he's natural or not, and I ain't about to look, if you know what I mean. About five foot nine—annoying voice . . . kinda mushmouthed, y'know. Not nice and decisive, like us! He wears these contact lenses. And that's about it. About the size of it."

"We will soon see the size of it," the woman said, and leaned in, and slipped the blade under Robinson's belt and slashed through the belt, cutting it in two.

"Sweet Jesus!" Robinson said, his sex life flashing before his eyes.

"His name," the woman said.

"Shit," Robinson said, in a panic, "I can't remember! You put too much pressure on even a strong man, and he can blank—he told me his name! But I can't. . . . Starts with an 'A' . . . I think. . . ."

"Take off his pants," she said.

The goons moved in, and several of them had knives, too; the pockmarked one was tugging at the captive's trousers, exposing the boxer's boxers.

"No!" Robinson yelled. "No, *don't* take off his

pants. . . . Adam! Andrew! Alan! . . . One of them white, frat-boy names. Oh, God—please don't cut off my penis! I'm attached to it!"

An explosion jolted the room—and Robinson, and his captors—as a door ripped off its hinges from the blast, and Alexander Scott charged in, firing, a pistol in either hand, like Butch Cassidy and the Sundance Kid rolled into one, taking on a million Mexicans. . . .

Around him, Robinson saw each of the goons pitch dead to the floor, blood splashing, weight thudding, their weapons clutched in useless hands; but when Scott turned toward the beauty, she bared her teeth in a snarl and deftly kicked first one, then the other pistol from his hand, and then flew at him, tackling him, taking him down. . . .

Robinson hopped to his feet, and slammed himself to the cement, splintering the chair; he shook the remains of it off, clawing out of the now-loose ropes, pulling up his pants, spying one of Scott's pistols, where it had fallen near one of the deceased goons.

Scott and the beauty were on the cement, wrestling, a provocatively sexual tussle that the male seemed to be winning, until the female's right hand found that other handgun she'd kicked from Scott's grasp. The dark beauty was trying to bring it around to shoot his head off, but Scott had her forearm, struggling to keep that barrel from taking aim.

And in the midst of that scrap, Scott's eyes met Robinson's—the fighter was standing there with the other pistol in hand.

"Shoot her!" Scott yelled. "Damnit, shoot her!"

Only Kelly Robinson was a ring warrior, not a trained assassin, like Alexander Scott; and he hesitated. . . .

But only for a moment.

Kelly Robinson took aim, but then closed his eyes, turned his head and did the distasteful business of squeezing the trigger. . . . He heard the deafening bang, and then the sickening thud of a body hitting cement.

And when Robinson opened his eyes, the beauty who had so adored his scent lay dead next to a very much alive Alexander Scott.

"Holy shit," Robinson said.

Getting to his feet slowly, Scott said, "You okay?"

Robinson was breathing hard, shaking his head, wishing this nightmare would leave him. "Holy shit," he said again. "Scotty . . . is she dead?"

In response to that, the beauty rolled over and opened her eyes and sat up.

"No," she said.

"Jesus!" Robinson said. What *Friday the 13th* shit was this? He blasted away again.

Nothing—just the unpleasant shrillness of the gunshot careening off cement walls and floors.

He was about to try one more time, when the four goons also got up from the cement floor, grinning at him. Robinson whirled and shot at them, the gunfire ringing in the warehouse; but like zombies they kept coming. . . .

Scott said, "You can stop shooting now."

And the agent took the gun away from a bewildered, damn near freaking-out Kelly Robinson. "What the hell . . . what the *hell's* goin' on here?"

The beauty smiled, in a rather prim, business-like way, and extended a small perfect hand.

"Special Agent Rachel Wright," she said, the accent replaced by a faintly British one. "A pleasure to . . . *officially* meet you. And that *is* nice-smelling cologne."

"You're . . . you're a spy, too?" Robinson managed.

She winked. "Yes . . . but don't tell anyone."

"Anybody tries to cut off my dick, lady, yours is the first name I'll spill—*that* I promise you!"

Scott put a hand on his reluctant partner's shoulder. "I can see how you might be confused about this, Kelly. I mean, Rachel did practically rape you."

She looked at Scott, perhaps a little hurt. "I was just doing my job."

"Dirty job, but somebody has to do it?" Scott said to her. "You didn't have to enjoy it so much. . . ."

Scott seemed a little owly about this, to Robinson, who was just coming out of his stupor.

Looking around the warehouse, at the quartet of "zombies," the boxer said, "Hold up. . . . *All* you are BNS."

Nodding, Rachel said, "Alex wanted to try you out, before we put you into the game."

"Game," Robinson echoed hollowly. "So, then, this was, what? A test?"

"A little bit," Scott said.

"Shit, man! I almost had a damn heart attack!"

"Nah. Man in tip-top shape like you?" Scott grinned at him. "Anyway—you rocked, man!"

Robinson blinked. "I what?"

"Rocked. Aced the sucker."

Robinson breathed out. "I did?"

Scott squeezed his partner's shoulder. "Dude! I have seen hundreds of agents put through that same exercise . . . it's a sort of BNS pop quiz . . . and I have never seen it handled so well. I mean, you didn't crap your pants or anything."

"Yeah. Well, I guess that's somethin' to be proud of."

"I mean, when you said, 'He's blond' . . . pure genius. Give 'em just a little, to make 'em think you're cooperating. But you never gave 'em my name."

Robinson—relieved, complimented—said, "Yeah, well that just came to me. . . . You know, boom. My business, you got to be able to improvise. Strategy on the fly."

Scott patted Robinson on the back. "Well, it was excellent strategy, man."

"But I'm surprised it was a, you know, sting . . . 'cause it felt like the real deal." He gestured to his groin. "See, when my guys are tingling, I know something's up. . . . *You're* in the spy business. You must know what I'm talking about."

"Not exactly," Scott admitted. "I have my own instincts, but my, uh . . . 'guys' stay out of it, mostly. But . . . every agent is different."

Robinson was into it now, and was moving around the area, gesturing to the site of the little psychodrama he'd just starred in. "See, I figured if I give 'em jus', you know, a few little kernels of the truth, that'd keep 'em guessin' for a while . . . and give you enough time to rescue me. Which you did. Almost."

"Almost," Scott said.

Rachel said, "We know this was rough—and we apologize. But we had to be sure you could handle the pressure of a real mission."

Robinson smiled, shrugged.

"And we got our answer," Scott said, patting the fighter on the back again. "You know what you are, my friend? You are a 'why not' man."

"Say what?"

Scott gestured to the air, painting an imaginary, and fairly unspecific, picture. "Y'see, there are 'why' men, and 'why not' men. These 'why' guys are a dime a dozen . . . useless . . . no imagination, sittin' around asking, why this, why that? But the few, the proud . . . they are the 'why nots' . . . the men of action. And you, Kelly Robinson, are clearly one of them."

Robinson—possibly giddy at just being alive, as well as still having his johnson intact—said, "I gotta admit . . . that's ringin' true. I mean, would the President of the United States've called me, if I wasn't the 'why not' type?"

"Absolutely not," Scott said.

"So," Robinson said. "When are us spies goin' to put our heads together, and talk about this damn mission?"

"Right this way," Scott said, and motioned to the doorway he'd cleared, not long ago, by blowing it off its hinges.

Robinson went on into the next room, while Rachel gave Alexander Scott a wry look.

Out of the fighter's earshot, he asked her, "Am I the puppet master or what?"

The beautiful woman in black leather rolled her eyes, and joined Robinson in the next room.

And Alexander Scott—thinking, *Let's see the great Carlos top* that *one*—tagged after.

6

....

Alexander Scott showed Kelly Robinson around the communications center and temporary HQ that had been assembled in the warehouse, a vast abandoned space BNS had acquired for this purpose. The small, corner room—the interrogation chamber where the little masquerade had been played out—was revealed now as a fake, a construction with the bare plywood walls of a film set.

Several banks of cutting-edge computers and com gear had been assembled, facing each other; the atmosphere was slightly surreal—the warehouse's ancient lighting bolstered by bright clip-on lamps, the dreary grays and browns of the building at odds with the crisply modern equipment.

As they walked, Scott said to the fighter, "What we're about to share with you is top secret—at the highest level of national security."

"Don't I need some kinda clearance shit for that?"

Scott smiled. "Oh, you were cleared by both the FBI and CIA before the President even called you. Your record as a citizen is exemplary."

"Yeah," Robinson said, grinning, "well, I try."

The truth was, Robinson's security clearance amounted to the following: the man paid his taxes, and had no arrests or convictions on anything worse than the occasional speeding ticket.

Still, Scott had been somewhat surprised by the man's file—the champ was a professional athlete through and through, and had lasted this long at the top because he trained rigorously and took his job seriously. For all his bluster, Robinson was a supporter of charity, and had established a summer boxing camp for ghetto kids enrolled in the Golden Gloves program. As a celebrity who'd sprung from impoverished beginnings, Kelly Robinson had not succumbed to substance abuse or any of the other temptations that a man in his position would be privy to . . . well, except for the ladies.

That, of course, had been the weakness Scott had played.

"Outside of the President," Scott told Robinson as they approached the bank of computers, "and a few key military personnel, no one in our own government even knows we're here."

"No shit?"

"None. You see, this is what's known as a black operation."

Robinson arched an eyebrow. "Well, hang onto your blond locks, Scotty, 'cause it's about to get a whole lot blacker. . . . Keep talkin', keep talkin'."

Scott ushered Robinson over to a computer—where one of the "goons" from the scam kidnapping, dark-haired, pockmarked Jim, actually a top BNS technician—sat at the keyboard.

Jim slid aside on his wheeled chair, as Scott and their guest—Rachel tagging after—moved in close on the monitor, on the screen of which was a photo of a familiar stark white-haired individual in his late fifties, tanned, smiling . . . a smile undermined by cold dark-blue eyes.

"This," Scott said, with a gesture to the monitor screen, "is Arnold Gundars."

"Looks like a pissed-off leprechaun."

"Don't be fooled—Gundars is a full-size, full-scale villain . . . the world's leading illegal arms dealer. And we believe he's in the possession of this. . . ."

Scott tapped several keys and brought up a display of a CGI representation of the Switchblade, positioned in front of a hangar with people and vehicles (also computer-generated) all around.

Robinson eyeballed the futuristically sleek, needle-nosed jet, its coloration a gray-blue, like gun metal. "A plane? You people made me think I was gonna get my dick cut off, over a *plane*?"

"Not just any plane, Kel—the Switchblade."

"Funny name for a ride."

Scott gestured toward the CGI image. "Has to do with the way the wings tuck in and then flare out . . . but also because of the swift, terrible damage it can do."

Robinson frowned skeptically. "That little bitty jet?"

Rachel stepped in alongside the champ, saying, "The plane is a highly sophisticated prototype stolen from the United States government three days ago. . . .

We know Gundars has it, and we believe he's not yet sold it. Our mission is to find it, and recover it."

Robinson raised a palm. "Hold up—we're the USA. And I ain't talking basic cable channel, neither. We're the best and brightest, right? We got radar and tracking and satellites up the whim-wham—you tellin' me we can't just, you know, *find* the sucker?"

Scott, frustrated by the man's ignorance, said, "Excellent question. Kelly, you're a natural."

Robinson shrugged. "I know. It's a gift."

"The Switchblade," Rachel said, "is the next generation of stealth technology—utterly silent, undetectable to radar, infra-red, sound, electromagnetic radiation . . . even the human eye."

"Silent but deadly," Robinson said. "I been there—try hangin' with my crew after an enchilada run."

Rachel leaned in and pointed to the image on the monitor. "The fuselage has a chameleon-like imagining system that digitally reads whatever is around it, and . . . 'paints' it on its surface."

Scott's fingers were poised above the keyboard. "Now watch, Kelly—this may only be a computer simulation, but it's quite accurate. . . ."

Then the secret agent tapped a few keys, and the Switchblade seemed to disappear, leaving only the hangar, the people and the vehicles.

"This is what the Switchblade would look like," Scott said, "with its optical cloaking device."

"It don't look like nothin'."

"Right."

The fighter was nodding. "I get it—it's like one of them bugs that looks like a leaf."

"Sorry, what?"

"You know, Scotty—one of them bugs. They just hang out on a branch all day, safe and sound, 'cause they blend right in—look just like a leaf."

Scott was nodding. "Good analogy."

And it was.

But Robinson wasn't content to leave it at that, saying, "I don't know why you guys called this plane the 'Switchblade,' in the first place. Shoulda called it the Leafy Bug."

"Well," Scott said, with a smile, hiding his real feelings, "I'll be sure to pass that along."

"I mean, this is just a prototype, right? Real deal could be the Leafy Bug."

"Could. Could."

Robinson's eyes widened. "Oh *shit,* man!"

The outburst jarred Scott, who said, "What's wrong, Kel?"

Robinson was looking at his wristwatch. "While we was playing your reindeer games, time's slippin' away. It's damn near eight o'clock! What the hell's wrong with you, Scotty? You wanna be late for the *mission?*"

Scott stared at the champ for a moment, then said, "You wouldn't be yanking my chain, would you, Kel?"

That dazzling smile flashed.

"Little bit," the champ said.

* * *

Within the half hour, Alexander Scott and Kelly Robinson were looking sharp in black tuxedos, Scott in a bow tie, Robinson a flatter, more stylish cross tie. Agent Rachel Wright was in a chauffeur's cap and uniform, and Scott found this butch apparel enormously attractive on her; of course, he realized he would have found her attractive in nothing at all . . . which maybe went without saying.

At the door to the warehouse, Rachel stopped to accept what appeared to be a gold ballpoint pen from the tech, Jim. Scott and Robinson were standing by the limo and did not hear the exchange between the tech and the lovely agent in chauffeur drag.

"Sat link is good for the next seventy-two hours," Jim said.

Rachel sighed, raised an eyebrow. "Thanks—let's hope that's more than enough time. . . ."

"Has to be. That's all I can give you."

At the limo, Robinson was inquiring about a backpack Scott held by one strap. "Black tie and backpack? That some kinda white thing?"

"I'm not taking it with me," Scott said. "Just a little insurance policy I'm gonna have stashed away . . . Bob!"

Another of the BNS agents approached and Scott handed him the backpack. "Set me up at the Siklo. Just in case."

The agent nodded, took the backpack, returned to the warehouse, while Robinson said, "In case of what?"

"Contingencies. Contingencies."

Robinson was thinking that over while Scott caught up with Rachel, before she got into the limo and behind the wheel. "Wait up!"

She paused, turned to him, her expression businesslike. "Yes, Alex? Problem?"

"No!" He gave her a shy smile, gestured rather fumblingly, and said, "Just . . . good luck.

"Actually, you and your civilian will need the luck. This is dangerous. I wish Mac hadn't . . . nothing."

Scott perked up; was she concerned about him?

"Isn't this weird?" he blurted. "Getting in a car, going off somewhere together—whole mission has the unmistakable feel of a stakeout, don't you think?"

"Not really," she said, wincing. "No."

"Good." He patted the air. "Good. Staying focused. Keeping sharp."

She granted him a smile. "Good luck, then, Alex."

The *you'll need it* seemed understood.

In the backseat of the limo, the secret agent and the boxing champ said little, exchanging occasional nervous smiles, now and then patting each other on the shoulder or knee.

Soon the limo was in a long line of cars—a Mercedes in front of them, a Trabant behind—waiting to get into the Royal Palace, on the long, narrow plateau called *Varhegy* (or Castle Hill), an area of cobblestone streets, well-preserved historic homes and museums. The storybook surroundings conferred upon the evening a certain unreality; but Alexander Scott knew all too well the reality of what they were hoping to walk into: a nest of terrorists.

Caught here in the queue of cars, Rachel removed the gold pen from her breast pocket and withdrew from a sidepocket a very special palm pilot. Turning the crown of the pen initiated a display—a map of Budapest with a red pulsing indicator dot on the palm pilot's LCD.

"And we are *live,*" Rachel said.

She handed the pen back to Scott.

"What's that?" Robinson asked, frowning.

Scott asked, easily, "What does it look like?"

"A pen. One of them fancy expensive ones."

Rachel, looking at them in the rearview mirror, said, "A limited edition golden Mont Blanc, a model Arnold Gundars prefers—carries one of these with him, everywhere."

Robinson's frown deepened. "How do you know that? Kinda pen a man uses."

"Our intelligence," Scott said. "We have great intelligence, at the BNS. . . . Right, Rachel?"

"Exceptional," she confirmed, and Scott admired that she'd kept a straight face saying it. "There's an IHB tracking device built into the chamber. I have a GPS map right here. . . ."

She held up the palm pilot.

"IHB," Robinson said, his frown turning confused. "GPS. . . . I suppose you'd have to kill me, if I knew what any of that stood for."

"No," Scott said. "Unclassified."

But he didn't explain.

Rachel was saying, "The idea is—Alex will plant this pen on Gundars. . . ."

"Pull a switch on the chump," Robinson said, following.

"Yes . . . pull a switch on the, uh, subject. Then we can follow our arms dealer's movements."

"Which'll lead you to your hot jet," Robinson said.

Tucking the pen into his inner tux jacket pocket, Scott smiled. "You catch on quick."

"Better believe it, jack."

They had finally reached the front of the palace, the *Kiralyi Palota,* a medieval castle looming in the night, awash with lights and flags.

"All right," Robinson said, the anticipation glittering in his eyes, "let's do this little thing."

The fighter got out first, then Scott, who leaned back inside to speak to Rachel, who glanced back at him from behind the wheel, hair tucked up under her chauffeur's cap, cuter than a box of puppies.

"Things are going pretty good so far, Rach," he said. "Don't you think?"

She gave him a slightly wide-eyed look, and—perhaps amused—said, "Yes, I do . . . 'Al.' "

His heart sank. "Was I too familiar, there? 'Rach' and all?"

"No. You'll do fine. So will Mr. Robinson."

"Thanks. . . . I just wanted to say, you look very nice this evening. I mean, you look nice every evening, but in that chauffeur's outfit, you're . . . I know it was designed for a man, and maybe you don't think it's all that flattering, but, hey—really works on you."

Now her amusement was unmistakable. "So— you're saying I look like a man?"

Panic coursed through him; why couldn't he have just gone ahead with the life-and-death mission? Why had he insisted on putting himself through this torture?

"Not at all, Rach . . . el. I'm saying you *don't* look like a man . . . *don't*. Even though you could . . . in that outfit, with your hair up . . . if a mission called for it. . . ."

"Why don't you go on into the party, Alex?"

"You know what? I think you're right. Never mind the other stuff."

Scott closed the door and turned, almost bumping into Robinson, who had clearly heard all of that.

"That's about the worst damn come-on I ever heard," the fighter said. "You *like* that fine lady? You're gonna need a better rap, man."

"I do all right."

"I doubt it. I bet you're jerkin' the gherkin more than Halle Berry's pool guy."

Scott sighed. "Let's just drop it, okay? Your only job here is to get me into this party."

They fell into a well-dressed line, tuxedos and furs and gowns and more jewels than Tiffany's vault; security guards dressed not unlike Scott and Robinson were using hand-held metal detectors to scan the entering guests. Knowing how many terrorists would be found inside, Scott could only question the efficacy of the process.

The night was cool, starlit, an almost full moon; wind played with fancy hairdos, but gently.

Robinson seemed annoyed. "Will you *look* at that damn thing?"

"What damn thing?"

The champ gestured to a large banner on one of the high ancient stone walls; it read:

FIGHT FOR THE TRANS-ATLANTIC CHAMPIONSHIP
ROBINSON VS. MILLS.

"Trans-Atlantic Championship?" Robinson said, horrified. "That's the pits, man. Don't even friggin' *rhyme*. . . . Who's editin' me behind my back? What the hell happened to 'The Slug-a-fest in Bud-a-pest'?"

"That is poetry. Sheer."

"Damn right it is."

"You seem to have a natural ability for naming things."

"Damn right I do."

"Great. . . . Now let's get inside this mausoleum and find the 'Leafy Bug.' "

Scott took Robinson by the arm and led him out of line and up to the front, where the guards in formal wear were doing their security routine.

"Excuse me," Scott said to one of the guards, who was between metal-detector scans. "This is Kelly Robinson, one of the guests of honor."

The guard—in fact, all the guards—brightened at seeing the famous face of the champ. The one Scott had approached took the champ gently by the arm, saying, "Mr. Robinson—welcome! I am big fan. Very big fan."

Robinson glanced back at Scott. "Lot of that goin' around."

Without being scanned, Robinson stepped on through the gate; and Scott began to tag after, but one of the guards grabbed him by the arm—not so gently.

Scott said, "I'm with the champ."

The guard looked toward Robinson.

"I never saw this guy before in my life," Robinson said. "If I were you, responsible for security and all . . . I would take him out back and shoot his uninvited ass."

Scott stared at Robinson in wide-eyed, open-mouthed disbelief, as more guards moved in; and then they were dragging him toward a security area, where several others had been detained. . . .

"Yo, yo, guys!" Robinson called out, laughing his distinctive horsey laugh. "I'm just playin'—the white boy's with me. My assistant."

The guards paused, then glanced at Scott, who grinned feebly, and then everyone laughed . . . almost everyone. That feeble grin was all Scott could manage, under the circumstances.

The secret agent raised his hands for a guard to give him a scan with a detector, the guard then waving him through.

Scott fell in alongside Robinson, who was already mingling with the dressed-to-the-nines crowd in the spacious cobblestone courtyard—it was an open-air reception; the spy glared at his grinning "partner."

"What the hell was that?" Scott demanded.

"That right there?" Robinson asked innocently; then his eyes tightened and he said, "That was for my hotel room. . . . Kinda wanted to even us up, before we do our mission. But you did great—didn't crap your pants or anything."

Pissed off, but (mostly) hiding it, Scott followed Robinson into the main party area, where guests congregating around a champagne fountain—seeing the honored guest approach—began to applaud. Robinson raised his arms, clasped his hands victory-style, accepting the praise wholeheartedly.

"Y'all ready," Robinson called out in jovial and typically cocky fashion, "for the Slug-a-fest in Budapest?"

Applause and smiles continued, but it was clear this crowd had no idea what the champ had just said, or meant anyway.

"You see our host anywhere?" Robinson asked Scott, meaning Arnold Gundars.

Waitresses in cleavage-generous peasant blouses and flowing embroidered skirts, and waiters in ornate red historic military uniforms and Cossack caps, were threading through the crowd with platters of hors d'oeuvres and champagne glasses.

"Haven't spotted him yet," Scott said. "But here's another warm human being. . . ."

A small Arabic fellow in a tux and a turban approached the champ with his hand outstretched. "Mr. Robinson—a rare honor to meet you, sir."

Shaking the man's hand, Robinson said, "Well thank you. It's an honor to meet you, too. Sir."

The Arab moved on, Scott watching him as the man disappeared into the crowd.

"Nice little fella," Robinson said.

"Big, in his way, though," Scott said. "That was Marwan Motaheeshi."

"Mota who?"

"Bin Laden's second in command."

Robinson's eyes flared. "*That* was a terrorist?"

"They don't wear name tags, Kelly."

"That little weasel? He seemed so . . . nice."

"I'm sure his mother loves him. See that one?" Scott indicated a passing guest in a tux, a harmless-looking Hispanic, also rather small of stature. "Felix Cesar . . . Cuban Nationalists. That smiling, freckle-faced guy? Patrick Callahan . . . IRA."

"Chuck Heston's second in command?"

"That's NRA . . . whole different deal." The secret agent casually, slowly, scanned the crowd. "Ah . . . here comes our man. Our host. . . ."

Gundars—of average height, distinctive in his purple nehru jacket, his snow-white hair thinning somewhat, wispy in the wind—had obviously spotted the champion and was making his way toward them, occasionally stopping to exchange polite party conversation with various of his guests. A trio of bodyguards in evening black trailed him, keeping a respectful—but easily closed—distance from their master.

Scott removed the gold Mont Blanc from his inside tux pocket; but Robinson snatched the pen from his grasp.

"*I'll* do the pen," the champ said.

"What?"

"Doin' my bit, Scotty. I'm the celebrity. Easier for me."

Scott put a hand on his partner's shoulder, and forced friendliness into his voice. "Kelly—your job was to get me into the party. You did that job. And you were great . . . your little joke aside. Maybe I had that coming."

"You had it comin', all right."

"You were the best spy ever—proud to work at your side, buddy. Now—just *give me the pen.*"

Scott reached for the golden Mont Blanc, but Robinson jerked it away, then tucked it inside his own inner tuxedo pocket. "Don't sweat it, man—I'm on it. Situation, under control. I'm a 'why not' guy, remember?"

"Oh God," Scott said to himself.

Gundars was approaching; and Scott stepped to one side, trying to blend into the party landscape.

"Mr. Robinson," Gundars said affably, his British accent light and charming. "Arnold Gundars. . . . So good to finally meet you—I have long admired your work in the ring, your combination of science and psychology, with a dollop of showmanship. . . . Not since Ali. Simply brilliant."

They shook hands, Robinson saying, "What can I say? You're a man who knows what he's talkin' about."

"And now this pugilistic performance promises to be one of the most exciting sporting events Budapest has seen in quite some time. Perhaps in all of Europe . . ."

"What can I tell you? I'm an exciting guy."

Gundars moved in closer and placed a fatherly hand

on the champ's shoulder; something nasty had edged into the smile, now. "I have only one regret—which is that I won't be able to root for you."

"Really? And why is that? You bein' such a big fan and all."

Gundars stepped away, gestured with a casual hand. "It's just that my loyalties—both personal and financial—lie with Mr. Mills."

Robinson's eyebrows climbed his forehead. "Oh, you bet on the other guy. Mr. Gundars, that was not a good move."

"It's more than that, Mr. Robinson. . . . You see, I own Cedric."

"Really? And I thought slavery was illegal, even over here."

Gundars chuckled. "I should say, I own his contract. There he is now. . . . Perhaps I can introduce you, later."

The arms dealer was indicating an angry-looking Middle European, obviously uncomfortable in his tux, standing at the center of the attention of half a dozen affluent partygoers; Mills had a trimmed goatee and hard dark eyes, which were staring over at Robinson right now, like unfriendly lasers.

Now it was Robinson's turn to lay a hand on his host's shoulder. "Mr. Gundars—you seem like a nice fella. If you invested in that slab of lard, I promise not to beat on him, too bad. . . . Say, you got a pen on you?"

Nearby, eavesdropping, Scott groaned, inwardly; *this* was Kelly's way in, with the arms dealer?

Gundars cocked his head, studying the champ. "A pen? What for?"

"Well, normally I write with 'em," Robinson said, sharing that huge grin.

Then the champ leaned close to his host, and nodded toward a striking dark woman, exotic, voluptuous, in a low-cut glittery green gown.

"When I was comin' in," Robinson said, conspiratorially, "that fine example of God's best work stopped me and, wouldn't you know it? Turns out she's a fan, too. *Big* fan. Whispered her phone number to me . . . and I wanna write it down. Wouldn't wanna forget that!"

Gundars seemed amused, in a pixie-like fashion. "Is that so?"

"Oh yeah," the champ said, and pawed the air dismissively, "happens all the time. Kind of a perk—maybe you get that, too, bein' a kazillionaire and all."

Now the host's eyebrows rose. "You don't mind if a woman wants to exploit your celebrity?"

"Not at all, Arnold—mind if I call you 'Arnold'?"

A smile twitched at the oversized gnome's lips. "Not at all, Kelly."

"Anyway, it's clear she's just another of a long line of ladies, lookin' for a real man. So tired of being left unsatisfied, night after night."

Gundars nodded toward the exotic beauty, now. "Kelly . . . that's my wife."

"Really," Robinson said, and his grin turned soft.

Christ, Scott thought.

"Huh," the champ was saying. "That's kind of a,

whaddyacallit, *faux paus,* on my part, ain't it? Fine-looking lady. You're a lucky man."

And now Gundars flashed his own huge grin. "Kelly—I'm joking. That young woman is, I'm quite sure, most eligible."

"Oh, you're *joking!*" Robinson turned to various guests around him, and laughed his horsey laugh. "Man is joking. He's a card! High-larious! Really very funny. Don't see that in a rich man all that often. . . ."

But in the shuffle of all this, the request for a pen had gone forgotten.

Witnessing this debacle from the sidelines, Scott decided to take the reins back; he helped himself to a glass of champagne from the nearby fountain, and approached the arms dealer and the champ.

"Excuse me, Mr. Robinson," Scott said, handing the glass forward, on a cocktail napkin. "Your champagne . . ."

"Oh. Well, thank you, Alex."

Gundars was eyeing Scott the way a mongoose studies a cobra.

Robinson said to his host, "This is my assistant. . . . He's new."

Scott said to Robinson, "I'm sorry to interrupt, but I promised one of those lovely ladies over there, by the fountain, an autograph of their favorite fighter."

"And I just bet that ain't Cedric Mills," Robinson said, grinning again. "Got a pen for me?"

Scott patted himself, and came up empty. "Sorry, sir."

Robinson sighed the sigh of the long-suffering.

"What kind of damn assistant are you, you don't even have a pen on you? You know people are after me for my autograph, all the time. What the hell's wrong with you?"

"I could have sworn I had one," Scott said. "Some lowlife must have snatched it from me."

Gundars stepped forward, saying, "Use mine."

"You have a pen?" Robinson asked, with feigned surprise. "I thought you said you didn't have a pen, Arnold."

"Actually, we never got around to that."

"Well thank you," Robinson said. Then to his "assistant" he said, "Now you see? Man's prepared. That's why he's powerful. Successful. Always ready."

Gundars plucked the pen from an inside pocket of the nehru jacket, and handed the familiar-looking gold Mont Blanc to Robinson. Using the cocktail napkin Scott had handed him, the champ signed an autograph and gave the napkin to his assistant, who slipped away.

Seemingly absent-mindedly, Robinson tucked the pen into his inside tux pocket, saying, "I don't know if he's gonna last—kind of an airhead, frankly."

Gundars arched an eyebrow. "My pen?"

"Oh! Damn. Now, who's the lowlife? I'm sorry." Robinson reached back into the pocket, making the switch with the homing-signal replica, which he handed toward Gundars.

"Here you go," Robinson said.

But in the hand-off, the pen accidentally fell to the cobblestones beneath their feet, the top popping off in the process.

Scott, from the sidelines, saw this, his gut tightening; the last thing in the world they needed, right now, was for Gundars to have a close look at that damn pen.

The arms dealer crouched, picked up the Mont Blanc, stood and did exactly what Scott had feared: examined the pen, frowning.

"That's a relief," Gundars said, finally.

"What is?" Robinson asked, with a nervous smile.

"It's an expensive pen. Glad it's not damaged." He replaced the top, and slipped the pen into his own inner pocket. "Just because I'm . . . well off, Mr. Robinson, that doesn't mean I throw my money around."

Scott could see Robinson let out his breath; but he couldn't blame the man—he was doing the same.

Right now one of those burly bodyguards of Gundars was edging up alongside his boss, whispering in the man's ear. Gundars's only response was a curt nod; but then he turned with a genial good-host's smile to his famous guest.

"If you'll excuse me, Kelly," Gundars said, "I have some business to attend to."

"No rest for the wicked," Robinson said, cheerfully.

"Yes," Gundars said, with an ambiguous twinkle, and disappeared into the crowd, trailed by his trio of well-dressed thugs.

Scott sidled up to Robinson, who frowned at him.

"I was doing just fine without your help," Robinson said.

"Oh yeah," Scott said. "I saw."

"Anyway, we pulled it off."

"Yes we did," Scott said, watching as Gundars approached the small Arab who had spoken to the champ, earlier. "Our host is heading off with Motaheeshi. . . ."

"What are they up to?"

"I think I'll find out." He turned to his partner. "See if you can create some kind of diversion for me."

"Diversion?"

"Just some kind of distraction."

The fighter frowned. "What kinda distraction?"

"Make a scene or something—you're a 'why not' guy, remember? Improvise. Call attention to yourself. . . . How hard for you can that be?"

And Alexander Scott went off to do some spying . . . alone.

7

. . . .

The courtyard had a heroic flair, with its statues of
savage lions and historic figures, an echo of harder,
perhaps nobler times. Something about that seemed
appropriate, even inspiring to Kelly Robinson, as he
made his way to where a boxing ring had been set up
in honor of the coming championship event.

Right now, as brittle laughter and cocktail conversation floated on the breeze, the guests in their finery
were crowded around watching an exhibition match
between a pair of local boxers, the Hungarian equivalent of ham-and-eggers.

Distraction time, Robinson thought.

Robinson vaulted over the red ropes into the ring
and the sparring partners—immediately recognizing
the world-famous fighter—froze in mid-swing, their
eyes huge, jaws gaping.

"All right, fellas," Robinson said, grinning ear to
ear, his voice ringing through the courtyard, "play-
time's over . . . out ya go!"

He motioned at them dismissively, like a grown-up
shooing pesky kids out of his petunia garden.

The muscular, well-built men, bodies pearled with

Eddie Murphy stars as Kelly Robinson, undefeated super middleweight champion of the world.

Kelly tallies yet another win on his arm after his victory in the ring.

Along with his success come the perks of fame and fortune, including his own jet and entourage.

When the president asks for Kelly's help in a secret mission to recover a stolen U.S. spy plane called the Switchblade, Kelly gladly takes on his new role.

BNS Special Agent Alex Scott (Owen Wilson) is less enthusiastic about his new partner.

Before the mission, Kelly undergoes a test of his spy skills, executed by fellow BNS agent Rachel (Famke Janssen).

To everyone's surprise, Kelly passes with flying colors.

On the eve of Kelly's boxing match, Kelly and Alex must infiltrate a formal party full of terrorists eager to purchase the spy plane for their own uses.

They manage to make contact with illegal arms dealer Arnold Gundars (Malcolm McDowell), who they believe has the Switchblade.

Together, Alex, Kelly, and Rachel try to track down the plane before it's too late.

Kelly finds being a spy more dangerous than he thought, as he works relentlessly on the mission . . .

. . . while trying to defend his career record at the European Middleweight Boxing Championship.

As a team, Kelly and Alex are each other's only hope to find the plane and make it out of Budapest alive . . .

. . . That is, if they don't kill each other first.

sweat despite the coolness of the evening, did as they were told, exiting the ring as if they'd been caught doing something wrong.

Robinson prowled the ring, hands on hips, Superman-style. He slowly scanned the crowds—all eyes on him, murmurs of excitement rippling across the courtyard—and called out, "Where is my man Cedric? Where is Cedric Mills?"

The response was almost immediate, people parting like the Red Sea to reveal Mills and a clutch of mostly female admirers; the challenger's little flock was standing perhaps fifteen feet from the makeshift ring. A drink in hand, the dark-haired, sturdy, trimly-bearded, rather simian Mills scowled toward the ring, but said nothing.

"Cedric!" Robinson said, with a delighted grin, as if he'd just spotted a long-lost friend. "There you are, Ced! Now put down that steroid shake, and get your fanny on up here."

Almost snarling, Mills yelled back, in a thick Central European accent, "I do *not* take the steroids!"

Throughout all this, the middleweight champion had been surreptitiously taking note as his partner in espionage melted into the crowd, allowing their white-haired arms-dealer host, Arnold Gundars, and his turbaned guest, terrorist Marwan Mataheeshi, to make their move.

"Oh, come on, Ced!" Robinson joshed. He kept the grin going full-wattage, and made sure his friendly tone was at odds with his words. "You ain't got no neck, or no trouser bulge to speak of, neither. . . . So it's either steroids, or you're just a damn freak!"

The crowd was greeting this in a mixed fashion—
some laughter, some displeasure, much confusion . . .
many of those who did speak English nonetheless
could not follow Robinson.

But Cedric Mills did, at least well enough to know
he was the butt of the famous fighter's jokes, and that
this large gathering was witness to these outrageous
insults.

After handing the drink to one of his lady friends,
Mills rolled like a tank toward the ring, and jumped
over the rope, depositing himself inside, fists at the
ready, glaring at the man he would fight twenty-four
hours hence. The partygoers clapped and hollered, anticipating a free show; and perhaps Mills knew he had
made a mistake taking Robinson's bait, because he remained poised by the ropes, a tentative visitor inside
the ring.

Then, still wearing that wide grin, Robinson came
over with his arms spread, and, in a voice that could be
heard all across the courtyard, said, "Ced, you're a
good sport! . . . Let's show these nice people we're
professionals. We don't have any grudge, do we,
Ced?"

And Robinson extended his right hand, for Cedric
to shake.

Confused, Robinson's opponent didn't know what
else to do: he shook the champ's hand; and then suddenly Robinson had moved alongside him, slipping an
arm around his shoulder, chummily, walking the challenger to the center of the ring.

Calling no particular attention to themselves, Gun-

*dars and the Arab—casually chatting—disappeared
inside a doorway of the baroque palace, followed by
one of the tuxedoed thugs. That entry, however, was
unguarded—there were dozens of doors, after all, into
the castle-like palace, which was a series of massive
interconnected structures. And, anyway, all of the security guards in the courtyard had moved up along behind, and even into, the crowd watching Robinson's
carnival show.*

"Cedric," Robinson said, entertaining Gundars's
guests, his arm still around his confused challenger's
shoulder, "y'all shouldn't be gettin' your hopes up,
y'know . . . 'cause it really ain't gonna be much of a
fight."

Eyes blazing, Mills shook himself free from the
champ's grasp. "We will see about this!"

Robinson did a mock shiver. "Ooooh, that was ominous, Cedric. You know that word, Ced? Ominous? It
sorta means . . . *boo!*"

Mills reared back.

"See, Ced, like *that* was ominous. Case you were
wonderin'."

*Robinson, his attention seemingly on Cedric Mills,
noted Alex slipping unnoticed inside that same door
the arms dealer and terrorist had entered.*

In the meantime, the Hungarian boxer was trem-
bling with rage.

"Ah, Ced, lighten up, my man. . . . Ya know, I usually make a prediction about what round I'll knock a
guy out in. But I'm a guest in your country." Robinson
turned his taunting smile on the crowd, now. "So I'm

gonna repay this hospitality by givin' Ced here the opportunity to make his *own* prediction. . . ."

Mills gazed at Robinson with cold hatred in eyes so dark they seemed black, like a shark's.

"Ced, buddy, what round do *you* think I'll knock you out in?"

That elicited both laughter and outrage from the crowd.

Mills sneered. "Jokes . . . stupid jokes. You stop the jokes, or I will stop them for you."

"My, Cedric, but you are a funny man. You are highlarious . . . don't you think so, folks?" Robinson pinched the other fighter's cheek. "Ain't he just adorable?"

Mills drew back, furious.

"You know," Robinson said reflectively, "I like Ced here so much, I almost don't wanna beat him senseless, tomorrow night."

Mills shook a finger at the champ. "You will stop—"

Robinson slapped the finger away—playfully.

"Come on, Ced—let's build the gate up a little. Give the people a little preview of tomorrow night. . . . Nothin' serious, little open-hand sample. . . . Let's go."

And Robinson slapped the challenger—lightly—on his bearded face.

Stunned, humiliated, Mills brought his hands up, in fists, his face flushed.

"Look at Ced, gettin' all red. . . . I thought you people wasn't communists, no more. . . ."

And now Mills slapped Robinson. Not so lightly.

The champ slapped him back.

This process was repeated, the sounds of the slaps echoing across the courtyard like gunshots.

Now fists were raised, and the two warriors were squaring off, as security guards leapt into the ring, breaking it up, Mills ranting, raving, as both boxers were escorted firmly but respectfully from the ring, in opposite directions, Robinson now uncharacteristically silent, the source of his smile a secret one.

Then the middleweight champion of the world moved into the crowd, nodding, smiling, working his way toward the doorway where his partner in spying had entered.

Alexander Scott trailed Gundars, Mataheeshi and the bodyguard down a wide, opulent hallway, the secret agent's footsteps helpfully silenced by a plush carpet. He waited outside the doorway of the room into which they'd disappeared, but the thickness of the typically ornate door prevented any eavesdropping.

In fact, when Scott finally made out voices, and footsteps, and then a vaguely familiar series of *clicks,* he realized the trio was about to exit, and he darted across the hallway and ducked into the recess of a doorway, tucking himself there, barely making it before Gundars, his guest and the goon in formal wear walked casually out of the room and down the hallway . . .

. . . and not past Scott, thank God.

Gundars was saying, "You'll be notified tomorrow. . . . I have to be fair to all of my clients. . . . I'm sure you understand."

Then they were gone.

Scott emerged from his hiding place and returned to the room from which the three had exited; he tried the knob, and found the door unlocked. *Better to be lucky than smart,* he thought, and began to ease the heavy door open, getting a view of an expansive, dark-wood study-cum-library, walls lined with leather-bound volumes.

If intelligence could be trusted, this would be Arnold Gundars's inner sanctum, and the computer (its monitor screen glowing) on the massive desk in the center of the suite very well might hold the answer to the question of the hour: the location of the stolen Switchblade.

He considered going in, but the thought of that familiar sound—that series of clicks—stopped him. Was that the sound of fingers typing a security code onto a keypad? Had some kind of alarm system been invoked by their host, on his way out of this unlocked study?

Scott touched a hand to his chin, and then a hand, *someone else's hand,* touched his shoulder . . .

. . . and the secret agent whirled, ducking low, throwing a swift right hand at the shape behind him; Scott caught a blur of tuxedo and assumed this was one of the monkey-suited thugs.

But his assailant deftly ducked the blow.

Only, it wasn't an assailant: it was Kelly Robinson, rising in a fighting stance now, eyes hard, nostrils flared.

Scott sighed, stood. "What the hell are you doing, man?"

Robinson, slightly embarrassed, dropped his hands to his sides, and the fists fell into fingers. "What the hell are *you* doin', man?"

"You were supposed to wait for me in the courtyard."

Robinson shrugged. "You didn't say that. You said create a distraction. I distracted . . . when I was done, I come to back you up."

Like a ref counting out a fallen fighter, Scott cut the air with a finger. "*Never* sneak up on a spy. You can get killed that way."

"You can get killed throwing punches at Kelly Robinson, fool—fifty-seven-and-oh, remember? . . . Is that our host's study? Bet that computer knows a thing or two. . . ."

Robinson started toward the open doorway and Scott stopped him with a hand on the arm. "No, Kel— I think the security system's on."

The boxer looked at the spy with a you're-kidding-me grin. "Door's open, man—security system was on, there'd be bells ringing and dogs nipping our asses and shit."

Scott held out his hand. "Give me a cigar."

Robinson frowned. "What the hell makes you think I got a cigar on me?"

"No offense, but you're rich and pompous and annoying." Scott shrugged. "You *must* smoke cigars."

"Now that's messed up, that's some kind of reverse snob shit, damn discrimination, the way you assume stuff like that. And *you're* the annoying one—whiny, mush-mouthed cracker-ass. . . ."

But Scott was still holding out his open palm.

Half a frown dug a dimple in Robinson's cheek as he begrudgingly withdrew a cigar, and then a silver lighter, from his tux suitcoat's inside pocket.

"Just for the record," Robinson said, "*I* ain't the annoying one."

Then he handed the cigar to the secret agent, lighter too, and watched with mild amusement as it took thirty seconds for the blond spy to get the fat Havana going.

Once he had, however, Scott knelt and blew a stream of smoke into the study; like steam it rolled across the floor, making clear a solid plane of green laser light, just beyond the entryway, hovering one inch off the oriental carpeting.

Robinson was smiling. "That was cool. I admit it . . . that was some cool spy shit."

Scott said, "You better stick with me, now."

"Look at us," the fighter said, enjoying himself, gesturing to the tuxes that almost made each a reflection of the other. "Looks like we oughta be heading to the damn bacharach table."

"That's baccarat." Scott was barely listening, having a hard look at the study—specifically the high-domed ceiling directly above the desk with the computer.

In a fairly credible Sean Connery impression, the boxer was saying, "Robinson. Kelly Robinson."

"This is not a game," Scott reminded him, putting the cigar out on his shoe, and slipping the smoke into his pocket. "The next fan club that ties you in a chair and wants to whittle on your woody won't be fooling. . . . You want in on this or not?"

Dead serious, Robinson said, "Damn right I do."

"Then come with me. . . ."

Scott knew the way to the roof—the intelligence on that subject, at least, had been solid; they had paused at the window that gave them passage onto the stonework rooftop, Scott sitting on the floor of the sitting room they'd invaded, to remove his shoes and socks.

"Ain't no time for this-little-piggy, man," Robinson said, astounded. "What's up with this shit?"

Scott had his socks off, and the black shoes back on, now; and he handed one of the socks to Robinson, keeping the other for himself.

"Pull it on," Scott said, meaning the sock. "It's a mask."

Robinson held the sock between two fingers, distastefully. "Man, why do I have to wear your cheap smelly-ass sock over my million-dollar face?"

"Because mine have eye holes," Scott said, "and your hundred-dollar silk ones don't stretch."

They sneaked across the roof, surrounded by looming naked statues and elaborate stonework, keeping low, the masks covering their heads but leaving their eyes exposed.

Robinson was still bitching. "You got some serious foot B.O. working there, 'spector Gadget. . . . I'm takin' this sucker off—nobody can see us up—"

"If a guest does happen to look up," Scott interrupted, as they stopped, crouching near the domed skylight window, "I want them to say, 'Oh my God, there's somebody up on the roof!' "

"Why would you want 'em to say that?"

"Because it would be so much better than, 'Oh my God, there's world-freakin'-famous Middleweight Champ Kelly Robinson up on the roof!' "

Robinson saw the secret agent's point. "I just hope nobody says, 'Oh my God, there's Kelly Robinson up on the roof—wonder why he's wearin' that smelly-ass sock on his damn face'. . . ."

"I doubt they could smell it from down there."

"Don't bet on it. . . ."

But this seemed half-hearted, trailing off as the fighter watched the spy remove what seemed to be a cell phone from a tux pocket.

"This ain't a good time for phone sex, Scotty. . . ."

Scott said nothing, removing from the undercarriage of the apparent phone a rolled-up length of titanium mono-filament, with a small hook.

"What's that?"

Scott again said nothing, securing the hook to the metal window frame, making sure it was well-anchored to the roof.

"What the hell you doin', man?"

Scott opened the skylight window. "For the record, *you* are the annoying one."

Holding onto the "cell-phone" handle of the device, flicking a switch on it, Scott—he had removed the stocking mask, for comfort—lowered himself down into the dark study.

He had all but forgotten Kelly Robinson, who had

pulled off his mask too, and watching the spy with open admiration, whispered to himself, "Cool."

Scott stepped down onto the top of the large desk—the laser security system no threat at all, up here. He sat on the desk like an Indian, swung the monitor to him—the computer was already on—and, taking the keyboard, immediately got to work.

Come on, baby, Scott thought. *Tell Poppa where the plane is. . . .*

A log-in screen filled the monitor, and he looked around the desk to see if the arms dealer had his password scribbled or posted anywhere.

No such luck.

Then Scott began trying the list of potential Gundars passwords that intelligence had provided him; Scott had memorized the lengthy list, and he was only a few tries into it when he heard movement . . . *above* him!

It was that idiot Robinson! Hauling the handle up, pulling the filament by hand.

Harshly, Scott whispered, "What the hell are you *doing*?"

Fishing the line back up, Robinson pushed the button on the "cell" handle, so that the line retracted into the device.

"Stop it," Scott said, looking up from the computer at the figure framed in the skylight window.

"I'm comin' down and backin' you up, man," Robinson said. "Suppose somebody comes in on you—Kelly Robinson's *there* for you. . . ."

And the champ in the tuxedo began lowering himself down, just as Scott had.

"No, no," Scott said, almost whimpering. "Do *not* come down here. . . ."

But Robinson kept on coming.

Shaking his head, distracted from his job, Scott said, "You are impossible! You don't listen!"

Robinson, about half-way down now, had paused, but not because of Scott's admonitions; his features were tight, and he was looking toward the door.

"*You* better listen, man," the champ said, alarmed. " 'Cause somebody's comin'."

Scott turned toward the doorway—Robinson was right, voices, footsteps. . . .

The secret agent scrambled to his feet, standing on the desk, and jumped up, grabbing Robinson by the feet.

"Up," Scott whispered harshly. "Go! Go!"

Robinson pushed the retract button while the spy climbed him like a ladder, until they were both holding onto the cell phone, rising steadily toward the skylight.

They were only four feet or so from the window when Gundars reached an arm in, switched on the study lights, and quickly typed in the security code on a wall pad, shutting off the laser system.

Robinson let up on the retract button—silencing the gentle whir that would almost certainly have attracted the eyes of the white-haired man in the nehru jacket below. The two men, dangling like a big ungainly earring, froze in place—so close to freedom, and yet so very far. . . .

Gundars was in the company of a stocky uniformed

North Korean, who Scott believed to be General Zhu Tam, though from this angle he could not be certain. One of the security thugs in a tux accompanied them.

Gundars was leading the Korean to the computer. "The funds will be verified overnight," the arms dealer was saying, "and the highest bidder will be notified in the morning."

"But I must see the plane."

Gundars was entering his password. Scott tried to watch the man's fingers, but couldn't see from here; he and Robinson were suspended, swinging slightly, and the agent slipped an arm around the boxer's waist, hoping to steady them some.

Robinson gave him a look that said: *Don't get too cozy.* . . .

"I'm sorry, General Zhu Tam," Gundars was saying. "Only the highest bidder will have that privilege."

Scott had been right: this was the ruthless Zhu Tam himself.

"And it is really . . . invisible?"

This seemed to amuse Gundars. "Let me answer your question with one of my own: how long have you been in Budapest?"

"Why . . . three days."

Gundars gestured with open palms. "My friend, you have probably driven past the Switchblade a dozen times. . . . Now, if you would please enter your bid. . . ."

Zhu Tam approached the computer, typing numbers in, slowly, carefully.

"As you make your decision, on an appropriate figure," the arms dealer said affably, "might I remind you, General, that an undetectable nuclear delivery system would transform North Korea into a world power . . . overnight."

Another security guard entered, moving hurriedly to Gundars. The guard spoke quietly, calmly: "Sir, there's been a breach of security."

The two intruders dangling above heard this, and exchanged accusatory glances: *What did you* do? *What did* you *do?*

The smooth Gundars betrayed neither alarm nor anger, urbanely turning to his North Korean guest, saying, "Are you quite satisfied with your bid, my friend?"

The General half-bowed. "I am, sir."

"Good. I'm sure it's most competitive. . . . Well, thank you, General Zhu Tam." Gundars nodded to the bodyguard who'd accompanied them in. Then to Zhu Tam, Gundars said, "We'll speak again tomorrow. Always a pleasure."

"A pleasure."

And the bodyguard escorted the general from the study.

Gundars spun toward the guard who'd brought him the bad news, the arms dealer's fury now evident. "Where the hell was this breach?"

"Right here in this room, sir. Silent alarm triggered."

Gundars wheeled, looking all around the study. "Could be the lasers . . . but nothing seems disturbed. Or it could be. . . ."

And now he looked up.

But by this time Scott and Robinson were scrambling up and scurrying out through the skylight window.

The guard below raised a pistol and might well have nailed one of them; but Gundars grabbed the man's arm, pushing it down, saying harshly, "Not without a silencer, you fool—our guests? The party? . . . Give me your radio."

Their masks back on, Alex Scott and Kelly Robinson were already dropping down from the dome level onto a lower back area of the roof. They had barely done so when something kicked at their feet . . .

. . . *silenced gunshots!*

The two men dove behind a pair of classical statues adorning the roof's portico: a man wearing only a figleaf unashamedly facing a shapely naked venus; Robinson hid behind the former, Scott the latter.

More bullets flew, deadly whispers turning pieces of the statues to powder. Ducking, Scott braced himself on the naked woman's well-rounded posterior; a moment later, struck by an absurd sense of decorum, he released his grasp, saying, "Sorry," reflexively.

Crouching behind the naked male statue, Robinson's eyes were wide and frightened in the mask's eyehole, as he peeked around to look at the shooters.

"Don't suppose," Robinson said, "this is another of your wacky tests, huh?"

Suddenly the female statue received some unnecessary unrequested surgery: a nine-millimeter breast reduction.

"That ain't no test," Robinson said, answering his own question.

A series of bullets—the sound of the stonework getting chewed up much louder than the gunshots themselves—carved terrible gouges in the two statues, disfiguring them grotesquely.

In moments, the same could easily have happened to the two spies hiding behind the figures . . . though without the possibility of future restoration by artisans. . . .

Keeping low, Scott made his way to the edge of the roof and had a look—the tan canvases of several catering tents stretched out below, a four-, maybe five-story fall. He motioned Robinson over.

"We gotta jump," Scott said.

Silenced bullets whined, carved up stone.

"You are one crazy caucasian."

"Got a better idea, Champ?"

"No—you're the secret agent; you're the one with the contingencies. Better come up with one, 'cause I ain't jumpin'. That shit, I don't do."

"Okay. New plan . . . stay right there . . . don't move."

Scott, keeping low, moved back behind the statues.

Robinson looked at him curiously.

Then the secret agent was running right at him, and Robinson was just rising, to get away, when Scott whammed into him, tackling him, carrying him off the roof.

It happened so quick, Robinson didn't even cry out—they just went sailing off the edge of the palace and fell eighty-some feet, onto the billowing folds of the catering tents, as if from a burning building onto a fireman's net.

If they had expected to bounce, however, they were wrong: the canvas ripped under their impact, as the two men came crashing down and through; and then the partially collapsed tent landed on startled, scurrying waiters, and on top of chefs, too—pots and pans, food and glasses, were scattered every which way, clattering, shattering.

The catering staff was yelping around them as the spies hit, hard, on a banquet table, which slammed to the floor under their wallop.

"See," Scott said reasonably. "That wasn't so bad."

And Robinson, underneath the secret agent, groaned, "Yeah, for *you* . . . 'cause I broke your damn fall."

The partycrashers climbed to their feet, and Scott yanked his stocking mask off, and then reached over and did the same with his partner's, tossing them.

"Take off your jacket," Scott said.

Robinson glanced around, noting that some of the catering staff—still darting about like beheaded chickens—wore white shirts and ties and black trousers. Getting his partner's point, Robinson threw off his tux jacket, and gestured to the table they'd just toppled.

Now it was Scott's turn to get his partner's point, and moments later, the pair exited the demolished tent holding up trays of food, in the process hiding their faces from security guards who were streaming in toward the palace.

"Now what?" Robinson whispered.

"Rule number one," Scott said. " 'Never enter a site unless you've got a sure way out.' "

"Well, I'm glad you got around to 'rule number one' here on the ass-end of the mission."

But the two men did all right, getting a fair distance before a guard called out to them.

"You there! Halt."

Robinson looked sideways at Scott. "Now what?"

"General rule . . . *run*."

The two "waiters" dropped their trays and did that very thing.

8

· ·

Behind them, the shouts of guards alerting other guards, in both Hungarian and English, provided inspiration to the two spies, as they ran at breakneck speed through the palace gardens, alarming clusters of startled guests, who scattered out of their path like self-propelled bowling pins.

The gunfire around them again whispered, though the potted plants the bullets shattered were not so polite about keeping quiet. No question about it: Kelly Robinson and Alex Scott had spoiled the party, and brought the wrong kind of attention to Arnold Gundars.

Robinson could tell Scott knew the layout of the grounds, that the secret agent had been prepared for this mission, so the fighter stayed at the agent's side, unquestioningly following his lead.

At least, Robinson did, until he saw Scott stuffing some chewing gum in his mouth. . . .

"Glad to see it," Robinson huffed sarcastically, as they ran.

Scott, working on the gum, gave his partner a sideways glance.

"That you can chew gum and run at the same time," Robinson said.

As for Scott, he indeed did know his way around the palace grounds—assuming this intelligence wasn't as sucky as on his last assignment—and he wound through the lush gardens until he came to the steps to the iron gate to the Siklo, the little dual cable cars leading up and down Castle Hill.

When they reached the top of the stairs, Scott found the gate locked; and all the while, the quiet gunshots were ricocheting loudly around them, carving stone, stirring up dust, nicking iron.

"Please tell me this ain't your sure way out," Robinson said.

"It's the *way* to the sure way out," Scott said, chewing his gum, pushing a putty-like plastic-explosive compound into the keyhole. He stepped back, blocking the boxer protectively, as a small blast blew the lock.

The pair went through, and Scott removed the gum from his mouth and stuffed it along the charred lock, then pulled the gate closed, re-locking it in his own way.

Ahead of them were the two little electric cable cars—funiculars—side by side on steep parallel tracks, cut overhead by a pair of pedestrian bridges; the quaint funiculars—fashioned of rich varnished wood and many windows—each had three small box-like compartments for riders to stand and enjoy the view (coming up) of Castle Hill, and (coming down) of the Danube; the compartments had a stairstep look and vaguely resembled a train engine.

Had they not been the object of armed pursuit, the two men might have stopped to gape at the commanding, floodlit nighttime view—the stately arches of Chain Bridge, the mix of historic and modern buildings that was the skyline of Pest across the Danube.

They had no such luxury. The car nearest them was about to leave, and Scott ran up, threw open a mostly-glass door, and hustled in with Robinson on his heels; a handful of romantic couples and other tourists had already boarded, and viewed these last-minute arrivals with surprise and a little irritation.

When the glass of the funicular's many windows began shattering under silenced gunfire, surprise and irritation turned to shock and terror, as the tourists and even the uniformed driver piled off, scattering for safety.

Within the funicular, Robinson was staying low, down below the already shattered windows.

"*This* is your 'sure way out'? Didn't I see the driver bail out, already? Scotty, can you drive this thing?"

"I need you not to worry," Scott said, calmly, a zen teacher scolding an unruly pupil, "and to stay positive."

A bullet fragmented one of the few remaining windows, raining glass down on the crouching fighter. "Just *go!*"

Scott threw the lever to start the funicular—he had been fully briefed in its operation—and the car began its ride down the hill . . . at about three miles per hour.

"Hit the gas, man!" Robinson demanded.

"It's electric—we're at top speed."

Bullets were careening off the bricks and cement surrounding the tracks.

"I could *roll* down the hill faster!"

"Be my guest."

Half a dozen of the armed guards in formal wear, their silenced weapons in hand, were running after the slow-moving car, now—in seconds, it seemed, the pursuers were bound to catch up.

Scott reached up and undid the rooftop service hatch, and slid it back.

"Oh," the cowering Robinson said, "you figure they can't get a good enough *shot* at us, with the roof on! I get it! You're just bein' helpful!"

As if proving Robinson's point, the car was passing under the first of the two pedestrian bridges, and several of the guards were up on it, and their bullets streaked down into the car, through the open hatch, sending slugs ricocheting all around inside the funicular, the two men ducking, hugging walls.

Then the car had passed under the bridge, and the pair of guards ran down the stairs alongside the tracks, still in dogged pursuit.

Robinson, down on the glass-strewn floor, said, "Man, we are gonna die."

"I asked you before," Scott said, opening a bench inside the car, "to please stop being so negative."

The secret agent withdrew a familiar item—the backpack he had been given by that BNS agent back at the warehouse.

"Contingencies," Robinson breathed.

"Contingencies," Scott said, taking out several grenades from the backpack; he tossed two to Robinson, got two for himself.

"You're the man! Grenades! We'll blow their asses to hell and back."

"Actually, Kel, they're smoke grenades."

Robinson's eyes widened. "Smoke? They get bullets, we get smoke? Is that fair?"

"Just pull the pin and throw. You take the left, I'll take the right."

Robinson did as he was told, and hurled his two grenades, as Scott was doing the same, and within seconds the funicular was shrouded in smoke.

As the two spies held their breath, working under the cover of the fumes, Scott removed a folded yellow plastic square from the backpack, to which he attached two small canisters, also stowed in the pack. He turned a knob on either canister and the plastic square soon became round, as it inflated into a sizable balloon.

Scott pulled from the bottom of the canisters a pair of lightweight subway-style straps. The gunfire seemed to have stopped—hard to tell, as so many of the windows were broken, and the pistols were, after all, silenced—but it appeared their pursuers, unable to see through the smoke, were not wasting ammunition.

Holding onto the balloon handles, Scott and Robinson were lifted up through the hatchway and into the smoky air.

Coughing a little, but not minding—elated just to be alive—Robinson said to his partner, "I never doubted you, man! You're the best—I knew you had somethin' good up your damn sleeve!"

Higher they were lifted, into the cloud of smoke, concealed from their confounded pursuers below.

"You know, Scotty," Robinson said, "I think I'm kinda warmin' up to you."

"Thanks," Scott said. He was gazing down through the thinning smoke. "This is one of those rare, male-bonding moments. . . ."

"In a very heterosexual way."

"Very."

Higher. . . .

"So. Scotty. You know some way we can steer this thing? Maybe let the air out, gradual and shit? How do we get down, anyway?"

The balloon cleared the line of smoke provided by the grenades, rising into the cool, clear night sky.

Scott said, "I don't think we're gonna have to worry about getting down."

"What do you mean?"

Scott nodded, earthward: the guards below had spotted them, fingers pointing . . . *guns* pointing. . . .

"Oh, shit!" Robinson said.

"Stay positive, now," Scott said.

And a bullet ripped into the balloon, piercing its plastic skin, letting gas out in a sick whistle; then another bullet did the same, adding a second, discordant whistle to the painful music of their inevitable descent. . . .

The good news was that the escaping gas propelled the balloon quickly away from the men with guns, out of pistol range; the bad news was the balloon then ran out of gas, and—limp membrane that it was—allowed the two men to drop from the sky, sending them hurtling toward mother earth, though not letting go of the handles, the flaccid balloon trailing after them.

They were above Clark Adam Square, about to crash down in the midst of traffic, when the deflated balloon caught hold of an ornament protruding over the mouth of the Buda Tunnel, snapping their plunge to a sudden, rubberband stop.

Now—either man holding onto his subway strap— the pair dangled about ten feet above the roadway, as vehicles sped by beneath them, in and out of the tunnel, mostly small foreign jobs, Scodas and Ladas, but Scott realized even a clunker could kill you, when you fell from the sky and landed in front of it. Several taxis passed, but hailing them seemed out of the question.

"Go ahead," Scott said, as they swayed from their handles, the scrap of plastic hooked on the tunnel ornament.

Robinson frowned. "Go ahead?"

"Time it, and jump."

Robinson looked down at the steady stream of cars, which seemed to be moving along at a good clip. "After you—I follow *your* damn lead, remember?"

"Wait . . . look at this. . . ."

A car carrier approached, hauling sports cars; this would make for a higher, easier fall . . . and on top, a convertible!

"With me, then," Scott said. "Ready . . ."

The car carrier was almost under them.

"*. . . go!*"

And both men let loose of their straps, dropping feet

first, not making it into the backseat of the convertible, as intended, winding up rather like a pair of big ungainly hood ornaments; nonetheless, they had at least landed on that convertible on the carrier's upper level.

This time, however, Robinson had fallen on top of Scott.

Slipping off, Robinson said, "Now we're even," and they crawled up over the windshield and got into the front seat of the convertible. For a moment, they just sat there, catching their breath, smiling at each other, glad to be out of this jam . . .

. . . and then, simultaneously, they spotted three dark Audi A6's, speeding toward the car carrier, weaving in and around slower traffic; in the lead Audi, one of those thugs-in-a-tux was leaning out the rider's side, pistol in hand.

"Persistent bastards, ain't they?" Robinson said.

"I would say so, yes."

Robinson snapped his fingers. "Got an idea."

"Excellent. Staying positive. . . . What is it?"

But Robinson had already climbed out of the car; he was scooching along the metal structure of the carrier, and then reached underneath the convertible.

"What are you doin', Kel?"

"Unhooking the axel chain of the end car, here. . . . My uncle used to take me to work with him, when I was a kid. Showed me how to do this shit."

Then Robinson edged around and also unhooked the chain on the car directly behind their convertible.

Scott called back to him, over the rush of wind,

"That's interesting. . . . So your uncle transported cars for a living?"

Robinson hopped back in the convertible, on the driver's side. "Uh, yeah . . . sort of."

The carrier was making a left turn onto the brightly lighted Szechenyi Lanchid, the Chain Bridge, that stately beautiful suspension affair, busy with night-time traffic.

Robinson leaned down and checked under the mat, where he thought he might find the ignition key—he was right.

Scott gave him a look. "Uncle teach you that?"

"Oh yeah. . . ."

And Robinson turned the key, started up the convertible, and threw it into reverse, ramming into the car directly behind theirs . . . which rammed into the vehicle behind it, the end car.

Which did not budge.

Robinson tried again, slammed into the car behind him, but still did not get the desired effect. He shrugged at Scott, who right now was just along for the ride, and then floored the thing, pushing hard into the car behind, the convertible's tires smoking as the vehicle strained to move backward. . . .

Those Audis were closing in now, and silenced guns were no longer the weapon of choice: UZIs appeared in the hands of thugs leaning out windows, and automatic gunfire ripped through the night, bullets slamming into the steel of the car carrier and its cargo, sometimes kissing a chassis and leaving gray-lipstick

puckers, other times sending slugs careening and ricocheting.

Robinson and Scott, however, up on top of the carrier, were a poor target for the UZI-bearing tailgaters,
and the champ kept at his back-and-forward course,
until finally the last car broke free and went violently
bump- and thumping down the ramp, the rear of the
vehicle hitting the pavement, hard, upending itself.

The Audi nearest the carrier found itself facing this
upended vehicle and the driver tried desperately to
avoid hitting it, but time wasn't on his side and the
Audi slammed into the bottom of the upright car, caus-
ing it to tip over backward, falling on the Audi's grille
and hood and windshield.

Scott watched the two vehicles become one in a
crunching tangle of metal and said, "One down. . . .
My turn."

The secret agent climbed out of the convertible,
walking on the steel structure of the carrier, slipping a
small device that resembled a pager from his pants
pocket.

"This is how we do it at the BNS," Scott explained,
kneeling and placing the "pager" under the front axel
of the remaining car behind them on the carrier.

Hopping back into the convertible, Scott said, "Pull
forward, Kel—you've got four seconds, by the way."

"Don't have to tell me twice," Robinson said, putting it in drive, and gunning it.

The convertible pulled forward just as the bomb
went off behind them, a ka-*whooom* that sent the remaining car snapping up to attention in mid-air, before

flipping over and coming down on top of the second Audi, bug-squashing the interior of the car, squeezing the passengers down, making it difficult for them to shoot out the windows of the vehicle, with its new low-ceilinged design.

"Two down," Robinson said, "and not too shabby."

But the third Audi skidded and skillfully avoided crashing into the second one, driving around the disabled car, and zooming up behind the carrier again, back on the tail of the two spies.

"I told you," Robinson said. "Persistent bastards. . . . But now let me show you a little somethin' they didn't teach you at spy school."

Robinson reached outside the car and flipped a lever on the carrier marked OPEN. The back ramp came down, extending out into the street and sliding out on top of the tailgating Audi, pinning the vehicle there in a metallic fingers-on-blackboard screech, lodging onto the Audi's roof.

"Also not shabby," Scott said, smiling.

Robinson laughed his horsey laugh and gunned the car, in reverse, backing off the top ramp and onto the bottom ramp extension, under which that Audi was pinned—its driver and passengers frantically trying to do something about it with no success at all—and backed out over the trunk of the pinned Audi, then *whump*ed into the street.

The moment they hit the pavement, Robinson threw the convertible into drive, shooting the car forward, and around and away from the badly damaged Audi, which seemed to be humping the rear of the carrier.

Scott breathed easier, settling back to enjoy the night breeze blowing in, as they headed into downtown Pest.

"Easiest way to get a car off a moving carrier," Robinson said. "Not that that was anything my uncle ever had to do."

"Of course not," Scott said,

Then they were on the Pest side of the bridge, convinced they had lost their pursuers; they were taking an upgrade when Scott glanced back and—incredibly!—saw two of the damaged Audis coming after them . . . unsteadily perhaps, but inexorably.

"Can't believe it," Scott said. "They're still on us!"

"Man, I told you they was persistent bastards." Robinson floored it. "Like white boxers—for-shit talent, but they keep comin' and comin' and comin' at you . . . wear you down. It's annoying, is what it is."

The convertible took a corner, moving fast, and, just behind them, a big truck, moving slow, backed out and neatly, sweetly blocked the pair of crippled but tenacious Audis.

Scott had no idea where they were now, Robinson racing the convertible down dark narrow streets; then the champ cranked a turn, shooting down a street that deadended at a small cafe.

Robinson started to back out, but Scott put a hand on his arm, shook his head and said, "Come on."

"If you say so—you're the spy."

"You are, too."

But they were out of the convertible now, and Scott

was heading toward an old Vespa scooter, with a wooden box on the back, which sat out in front of the cafe, from which laughter and jazz could be prominently heard.

Scott climbed onto the scooter, Robinson getting on behind him, on top of the box.

"Hold on," Scott said.

"Hold onto *what*?" Robinson asked.

But the secret agent had spotted something between the cafe and the building next door, and—as the two crunched Audis came careening into the cul-de-sac, Scott gunned the Vespa and headed for that passage and then they were *whump-whump-whump*ing down stone steps, a long narrow flight down the hill.

Robinson was bouncing around back there, trying to hold onto that box, and barely succeeding. "Man, you're killin' my ass!"

"Think of it as training," Scott said, as they neared the bottom of the steps, a cross street presenting itself, a welcome sight.

Then they were on the sidewalk, and the narrow street—on either side, little two- and three-story buildings dating back centuries—seemed free of traffic.

"Don't see them," Scott said.

"I don't see nothin'," Robinson said. "My eyeballs fell out about half-way down them steps, when my brain was bouncing up against my skull."

And then, around the corner, came one of the wounded Audis, screaming down the street at them, as if the vehicle itself were outraged.

"Oh shit," Scott said quietly.

"Tol' you, man! Per-frickin'-sistent. What I'm talkin' about."

Scott opened up the throttle, darting across the street on the scooter, just missing the oncoming Audi, heading for another passage and, presumably, another flight of stone steps.

But the scooter had picked up so much speed, catching a huge lift of air, it cleared the flight of steps, flying, not bumping Robinson at all—just scaring the hell out of him (and Scott)—and landing, with a teeth-jarring, bone-rattling *whump* on the pavement below.

Robinson held on to the sides of the box on which he was perched, slamming down on the wood so hard it damn near shattered.

Veering into the street, Scott picked up speed, hoping to make a clean getaway at last; but one of the ruined Audis came roaring uphill at him, behind the scooter, and then the other one was right in front of them, bearing down, crushed grillwork grinning crazily.

"One in front!" Robinson said. "One in front!"

"Stop yelling in my ear," Scott said. "I see him."

Swinging the scooter around the oncoming car, Scott allowed the two vehicles to slam into each other.

"All right!" Robinson said, jumping up and down on his wooden box, slapping Scott on the back, "way to go, man!"

"Alex Scott," he said, grinning. "Alexander Scott!"

"Say your name, baby."

They turned onto a road along the river, the moon

reflecting silver on the beautiful blue of the famous Danube; Scott slowed, and a peacefulness, almost a contentment settled in on them.

That was when another Audi—an undamaged one—picked up their trail; then another, and another!

"Three whole new ones," Robinson moaned. "How the hell many cars they got?" The fighter shook his head in extreme frustration. "That sucker Gundars got the Budapest Audi dealership or some shit?"

"This is bad," Scott said.

"Yeah . . . yeah, I know it's bad. Finally got bad. It's been so good up till now."

"I'm on top of it."

"You're in *front* of it! They're shooting, and I'm the one in back!"

But Scott was heading into the center of town, where a rolling gun battle should attract the attention of police, and put an end to this nonsense.

"Trolley!" Robinson called out.

And indeed, up ahead, two trolleys were approaching each other on side-by-side tracks, about to pass like strangers in the night.

Scott put on more speed.

"Trolleys, I said! Scotty, are you *off* yours?"

"This may be a little tight now, Kel—"

"No . . . you're not . . ."

"We are."

They were heading right for where the trolleys were about to intersect.

Robinson held on. "Scotty, we're gonna make it, right? . . . Right?"

"Shhh," Scott said, hunkered over. "Concentrating. . . ."

Thanks to the slenderness of the scooter, Scott slipped between the two passing trolleys, leaving the Audis on the other side of the intersection, screeching to a stop to avoid the trams.

And when the tram cars passed, the Audi headlights illuminated the Vespa . . .

. . . on the pavement, on its side, front wheel still spinning, as if the two riders had been tossed somewhere.

Gundars's men piled out of their cars and began to search the street, to comb the entire area. They looked everywhere, but the foul, steaming sewer.

Which was exactly where the two spies had hidden themselves, down in the muck and sludge.

"You all right?" Scott asked his partner.

Water dripped; the smell was rank. But they were alive.

"Last year I made twenty-four million," Robinson said. "And now I'm standing in six inches of shit. . . . I been better."

The sound of the guards running around up there, feet pounding on pavement, continued.

Scott said quietly, "You really made twenty-four million?"

Robinson ignored that, standing on his tiptoes to look up out of the sewer drain. Across the street, one of the goons was directing several other goons. Gundars's men seemed to be everywhere.

Robinson sighed. "They ain't goin' away, not for a while, anyway. We're stuck down here."

"Could be a while. Try not to breathe too deeply—this methane gas can mess you up. Make you loopy."

"Great. How will I tell?"

"What?"

"When you get loopy?"

Scott looked around. "Let's find a dry place and sit down."

"Good luck."

But they did, some stonework that left only their feet in the sludge.

"So," Scott said. "Where'd you grow up?"

Robinson held up a hand. Politely, he said, "No, man . . . no offense. I like you. We're colleagues."

"Right."

"Maybe even friends."

"I hope so."

"But that's not really my thing—just not comfortable, openin' up and sharin' my personal stuff with another guy."

"That's cool, Kel."

"Cool."

"No problem."

Five minutes later, the two had their ties off and their shirt collars loosened.

"So," Robinson said, "it was really my grandma who raised me, after my mama died. My gram' taught me everything. Without her, God knows where I'd be—be in the shit, is where."

"Wow," Scott said. "She sounds great."

"I loved that ol' woman . . . till she went crazy on my ass and started beatin' the crap out of me. I swear, that old witch get liquored up, she could roll a newspaper tighter than a steel cable."

"Wow. Great."

Ten minutes later, the jackets were off and their sleeves were rolled up.

"Oh for sure," Scott was saying, "I've had a thing for Rachel for years. Man, you should see how she handles a knife . . ."

"I have, I have."

". . . and nobody, I mean nobody, can garrote a victim like Rach can. Holy shit, is that sexy."

"So, then," Robinson said, "you should go for it. You could get her, man."

"No. I can't. You saw me. I suck at small talk."

"Shit, man, nobody's talk is smaller than yours."

"Kel, with *her* I suck."

"You need to embrace your own wonderfulness, my man."

Scott raised his eyebrows. "The wonderfulness of my own self?"

"Abso-damn-lutely. Look at me! I came from shit. And look where I am now! In my own self-realized Kelly Robinson wonderfulness, I can have any woman I want. *You,* in your wonderfulness, can have any woman *you* want. You know why?"

"Why?"

"Because you are Meadowlark Lemon."

"I am?"

"Oh yeah. And I'll play Curly Neill to your Meadowlark, any day."

Scott was smiling, nodding, buying in.

Fifteen minutes later, stoned to the gills on methane, the two spies sat with shirts undone, their hair a mess, sweating, eyes wild—together in that special place where people share their darkest demons.

"I'm jus' a little boy, man," Robinson was whimpering. "Kelly Robinson is jus' a scared little boy."

"It's okay, man. I'm here for you, dude."

"It feels good to let it out, man." Tears were streaming down Robinson's cheeks—some of it emotion, some of it the effect of sewer gas. "It feels good to talk. . . . You tell me somethin' now . . . somethin' you never admitted to nobody."

Scott sat there quietly, for several long moments, staring into the darkness of the sewer.

"You won't tell anybody, Kel?"

"Not a soul, Scotty."

". . . The Gulf War?"

"Yeah?"

"I started it."

Before long, sunlight streamed in through the sewer drain, and two friends—brothers in sewage—crawled out of their confessional.

Kelly Robinson had a fight, tonight; and Alexander Scott had an invisible plane to find.

9

....

As dawn painted the cobblestones of the city, Alexander Scott and his new best friend, Kelly Robinson, returned to the Mecure Hotel Budapest Nemzeti. Robinson now had a suite—next to Scott's, actually—and the two men gave themselves three hours to shower the sewer stench off themselves, and grab a couple winks.

Scott, leaving Kel at his door, said, "I'm sorry about this—gonna be rough on you, a championship bout tonight and everything."

"Hey—don't tell anybody . . . but Kelly Robinson don't sleep much, night before a fight, anyway."

"You're not sayin' Kelly Robinson is *human,* are you?"

"Jus' don't let it get around, bro."

They clicked fists.

"You are my main man," Scott said, awkwardly, and Robinson grinned, shook his head, and took his smelly self, in all its "wonderfulness," into the suite to freshen up and rest a bit.

By late morning the pair had caught a cab to the seedy neighborhood where the makeshift BNS HQ had been erected in a warehouse. Scott, in a yellow corduroy jacket over a black t-shirt, ambled in with Robinson, in black leather jacket over a white shirt.

Rachel Wright, back in her own Emma Peel-ish black leather ensemble, rose from beside BNS tech Jim, at one of the computers, to rush over, wide-eyed.

"Thank God!" she said, looking from one to the other, obviously astonished by not only their presence but their casual, comradely demeanor. "Where have you two *been*? We thought you were dead!"

Scott shrugged. "We pulled a pretty good getaway, but Gundars unleashed all his big dogs. We were pinned down."

"Where?" she asked.

Robinson said, "Let's jus' say there was no shortage of food, long as your idea of a midnight snack is a rat-burger."

Scott explained that they'd stopped by the hotel, and Rachel scolded him for not calling in.

"Sorry—didn't have time to sweep the room for bugs," the secret agent said. "Trust me—you wouldn't be standing this close, if we hadn't taken the time to shower."

"Together?" she asked archly, noting the new chumminess between spy and fighter.

"Oh yeah," Robinson said, giving back as good as he'd got. "It was wet and wild, real soap-on-a-rope fest. . . . Wanna join us next time?"

Rachel ignored the sarcasm, and asked, "These men of Gundars . . . did they make you?"

"You got a filthy mind," Robinson said, then grinned. "I like that in a woman."

"She means, did they see our faces," Scott said to his partner; then to Rachel he said, "No . . . we were masked, at first anyway, and then we were up on top of this car carrier, and . . . just take my word for it. We're fine. We're okay."

"Well," she sighed. "I'm annoyed. . . ."

"He's very annoying," Scott said, gesturing to Robinson.

Robinson did the same, saying, "Guy is an annoying dude, what can I tell you?"

". . . but," she finished, a lovely smile blossoming, "I'm very relieved to see you. Both of you."

Scott smiled, shyly. "Well, thanks, Rach. . . . Been tracking our bugged Mont Blanc?"

Nodding, Rachel walked them over to the computer, where her small GPS unit was now plugged in, the monitor screen displaying the map with the red tracking pulse.

"The pen never left the palace," she said. "Gundars moved around the grounds and the castle itself, till around one-thirty A.M. . . . and the Mont Blanc has remained stationary in his bedroom, ever since. . . . Reasonable assumption is, he's not on to us."

Leaning in, Scott said to the tech, "Jim—let me know the second that pen is on the move."

"You got it," Jim said.

Now Scott turned to Rachel. "We've confirmed that the Switchblade is here . . . in Budapest . . . and that Gundars is closing the deal, today."

Her eyes tightened. "No clue as to the location of the plane?"

"Gundars teasingly indicated to one of his potential buyers that it's in plain sight, in the city." Scott called over to another tech, Bob, seated tending several monitor screens. "Bob, I want a copter in the air scanning every rooftop, playground, and parking lot in Buda and Pest. . . . Throw everything you've got at it, infrared, UV, the works."

"I'm on it," the tech said, fingers already flying.

Scott and Robinson wandered away from the bank of computers.

Robinson said, "Look at your bad self: you've embraced it . . . your wonderfulness."

With a quiet shrug, Scott said, "What can I say? They respect me."

"It's that commanding presence of yours, Scotty."

"Oh yeah. . . ." Scott was glancing over at Rachel, who was supervising the handful of techs manning the facing banks of computers.

"She feels it, too," Robinson said, slyly.

"My wonderfulness?"

"It's oozin' outa your pores, man. Go for it."

Scott took a deep breath, mustering his courage, and strode over to Rachel. "Uh . . . Rach?"

She turned toward him, business-like, but friendly. "Yes, Alex?"

"You look terrible."

She frowned; in the background, Robinson grimaced, and turned away, like a man witnessing a bad car wreck.

"I mean, you look *great,* but terrible . . . you know, tired . . . the *exhausted* kinda terrible."

Sighing, she shook her head, "Well, after all, I *was* driving around all night looking for you."

"You were?"

"Alex, it's my job."

"Of course it is. Look—you've been carrying the whole weight here, while I've been gone. Why don't you go lie down? I'll cover for you."

"If that pen moves . . ."

"I'll yell. Promise."

She sighed again, but smiling this time. "Okay. Thanks, Alex."

And the beauty in black leather entered the small corner room that had been erected for Robinson's "interrogation," last night.

Suddenly a hand settled on Scott's shoulder, and he glanced at Robinson, who said, "Way to go, Meadowlark—nice manueverin'. It's all set."

Scott frowned. "Oh no . . . no, no. I wasn't . . . I really did think she needed . . ."

"Didn't you see the way she looked at you? Didn't you hear the tone of her voice? That was an invitation to dine, my man—slip on your napkin and pig out."

"Well, that's very romantically put, Kel, but I'm *not* going in there."

Robinson hugged Scott's shoulder. "Sure you are. What happened to those contact-lens gizmos?"

The abrupt, seeming change in subject threw Scott. "Huh? . . . Well, I still have them right here, in my watch. Didn't use 'em last night, 'cause I didn't have a chance to properly train you in their use. We would've had several hours for that, on your jet, if I hadn't wound up flying us in, you know."

"Yeah. I was kind of a prick."

"Yes you were."

Robinson frowned. "You don't have to agree so damn fast. . . . Those contact lens, my friend, are your ticket to paradise." He nodded toward the closed door of the interrogation cubicle. "And the holy gates are right over there. . . ."

"Not going in. No."

"Oh yes you are. And you're gonna be devilishly charming, to boot."

"Devilishly?"

"Devilish as hell. And you know why?"

"You're going to tell me, aren't you?"

" 'Cause Kelly Robinson's gonna help you."

"How are you gonna help me? And what do the lenses—"

"Trust me. Alexander. If there's one thing Kelly Robinson knows . . . that *I* know . . . it's the ladies."

How could Scott argue with that?

"You just do what I tell you to do, Alex my man . . . and say what I tell you to say. No questions asked— and I will guarantee your success."

"Guarantee?"

"Double your money back."

"*What* money?"

Nonetheless, five minutes or so later, Alexander Scott slipped quietly into the interrogation room, where Rachel lay dozing on a small unadorned cot.

"Baby," Scott said, with the grace of a bear in snow-shoes. "You sleeping?"

The beautiful agent—her jacket was off, slung on a chair—leaned on an elbow and squinted at Scott as if he were out of focus; whether this was induced by drowsiness, or Scott's behavior, who could say?

He approached tentatively, hoping the listening device installed in his left ear was not readily apparent . . .

. . . as a rather gleeful Kelly Robinson sat at a table in front of a small microphone, near the computer monitor banks, wearing the receiving, monitor lens, closing his other eye, so that all he perceived was Alex Scott's vision of the lovely female agent on the cot, pert breasts apparent beneath a thin dark top, her legs under the black-leather mini skirt beautifully exposed.

Man, this is some kinda weird-ass virtual reality sex, Robinson thought, always ready for a new erotic experience.

Into the microphone, Robinson said, "I love the way your tongue flicks off your front teeth, when you hit the 'l'—Alex . . . Alex . . . Alex. . . ."

Dutifully, Scott repeated this, doing the tongue-flick thing as best he could.

Rachel did it better, when she said, "Alex . . ." But unfortunately she added: "*Leave.* . . . I'm sleeping."

He stood there gracelessly, listening to his next lines, regrouping, while she gazed at him as if he were a madman.

Finally Scott said, "All right—you want to sleep? Then I'll sing you to sleep, baby. . . . Close your lovely eyes. . . ."

Frowning, Rachel said, "What?"

In his ear, Scott heard Kel singing: *"Get up, get up, get up. . . . Let's make love tonight. . . ."*

Out in the warehouse, Robinson was not only singing, but out of his chair, dancing; but he could see, through the shared "eye," that Rachel had a horrified expression; and he could hear the deadly silence as Scott failed to follow the guaranteed Kelly Robinson lead.

"Scotty," Robinson said into the mike, "go on, man . . . trust me."

Scott drew in a breath, gave himself a what-the-hell imaginary push, and dove in, singing breathlessly, and rather tunelessly, "Get up, get up, get up. . . . Let's make love tonight. . . ."

And in his ear, he heard Kel saying, "And you're dancin' while you're singin' this, right? Please tell me you're not jus' standin' there—dance, baby, dance!"

So Scott began to dance—or something—swaying awkwardly as he continued to croon, "Wake up, wake up, wake up. . . . Helps you do it right. . . ."

And Rachel began to laugh.

Robinson could see through the mutual eye that the hottie was enjoying this terrible shit—she was *into* it!

"You're awful," she said to Scott, playfully.

After a beat to hear his prompt, Scott said, "Are you dissin' Marvin Gaye?"

"No, no," she said, her laughter like a wonderful wind chime, "I *love* Marvin . . . but you're bad."

Scott didn't wait for prompting: "Bad as in *baaaad*?"

"No," she said crisply, the faint British accent making it so sexy, "bad as in you stink. You call that a lullaby? A song that goes, get up? Wake up?"

Still on his own, Scott said, "Rachel, you're woefully out of step."

"Woefully?" she said, very amused.

"Oh yeah—this is what the kids are listening to, these days."

"Hasn't Marvin Gaye been dead for fifteen years—or is it twenty?"

"Rach! The kids like the classics. . . . It's what they groove to, to fall asleep."

Out in the other room, amazed at his pupil's success, Robinson smiled, thought, *Tap that wonderfulness, man, tap it. . . .*

Rachel wasn't laughing now. "Really? Kids have taste that good?"

"Oh yeah." He drew closer. "I would know. I make a point of staying . . . connected. Gotta stay hooked up to the world . . . baby."

I've created a monster, Robinson thought, laughing to himself.

"Also, music is my life," Scott said, and risked sitting down next to her.

She laughed again, warmly. "Music is your life?"

"Yeah! You saw me in that Weezer t-shirt that time, right?"

And she laughed some more, touching his arm.

In his ear, Scott heard: "She's laughing! She's touching you! We got her, baby . . . make your move."

Scott slipped his arm around the beautiful spy, and

she looked at him—and he looked at her—in a way, a sexually charged and yet romantic way, that was a first for them.

The voice in his ear, urgent now, said: "Repeat after me, man. . . . Girl, I'm gonna make sweet love to you, till you're beggin' me to stop and screamin' for more . . . all at the same time."

Scott heard all that, took it all in . . . but he hesitated.

The voice in his ear, calm now, said: "Scotty, say it your own way, man. Make it real. Make it wonderful."

And Scott stared into those lovely blue eyes and said, from the bottom of his being, "Rachel, I think I fell in love with you the first moment I saw you. I just thought . . . that's the most beautiful creature I've ever seen. Then we met, and you were funny and smart and, despite this rotten job we share, you had a good heart."

She studied him with sad, longing eyes. "You thought all that, Alex?"

"Yes . . . and I still do."

Out in the warehouse, Robinson was disgusted. Into the mike he said, "What the hell kinda Hallmark card bullshit was that?"

But then Robinson could see . . . as of course could Scott . . . the beautiful woman, her eyes moist, opening her arms to her shy suitor.

"Come here, Alex . . . come to me."

The voice in Scott's ear back-tracked: "All right, that's cool. . . . That sickening shit worked. We're in."

And Scott reached down to his wrist and clicked a button.

Out in the other room, Robinson's Scott-eyeview shut off.

The champ stood, frustrated. "Aw, come on, man— I did my part! Don't shut me out, now—'least let me see the goods!"

But Scott wasn't paying any attention to the voice in his ear. Rachel was in his arms, and he was kissing her, and she was returning the kiss, with a warmth, a passion he had only dreamed about, before this wonderful moment.

That was when the door flew open and the BNS tech, Jim, barged in. "Uh, sorry . . . but you said . . ."

"Yes?" Scott said, as he and Rachel broke away.

"The pen . . . it just moved."

Rachel was on her feet, grabbing her jacket from the nearby chair. "Let's go!"

Scott just looked at the tech.

The tech's expression was apologetic. "Sorry! I can't help it—the pen moved!"

The pen wasn't the only thing that moved, Scott thought, and said, "Good work . . . I'll be out in a second."

And the voice in his ear, laughing lightly, said, "What's wrong, Scotty? Can't you stand up?"

Within ten minutes, a nondescript blue car, of Hungarian make, swung out of the BNS warehouse headquarters. Alexander Scott was at the wheel, with Rachel Wright in the front rider's seat, as she monitored the hand-held tracking unit, watching the red dot on her small screen as it moved. In the backseat, but sitting up, was the newbie spy on the block: Kelly Robinson.

"Okay," Rachel was saying, "looks like Arnold's out of his car, on foot . . . heading for . . ."

"Where?" Robinson said, impatiently.

The beauty in black pressed a button, and the GPS zoomed in on a map of the area, so close-up each building was labeled.

Looking over her shoulder, Robinson said, "Some fly spy shit. Boxing don't come with such cool toys."

"He's headed for the Gellert Hotel," Rachel said.

"What's he need a hotel for?" Robinson asked.

"Maybe he's going to the baths," she said.

"What's he need a bath for?"

Scott said, "The Gellert Hotel is famous for its spa, its thermal baths . . . and you don't have to be a guest there to use them."

"Who cares?" Robinson said, shrugging. "As long as he ain't goin' shopping for a new pen, we're cool, right?"

Behind the wheel, Scott was frowning in thought. "But our intelligence doesn't say anything about the baths being part of Gundars's routine."

Rachel looked at Scott with an arched eyebrow. "But our intelligence sucks, lately, remember."

Robinson leaned up. "It does? . . . Hey man, you said the BNS had the best intelligence goin'!"

"That was the BS part of BNS," Scott said. Then to Rachel he said, "It is a public place—not bad for meeting with his potential buyers. . . ."

Rachel wasn't getting it. "Arnold couldn't be hiding our plane in the *baths,* could he?"

"Don't be so sure," Robinson said. "They don't call that baby the Leafy Bug for nothin'."

The Gellert Szalloda es Thermal Furdo, on Szent Gellert Square, was a cheerfully decadent art nouveau wonder, five weathered stories of sandy gray soapstone near the foot of the Szabadsag Bridge in Buda. It was said that the first settlers along these Danube banks, thousands of years ago, were attracted by the natural hot springs. The Gellert was only one of over a dozen historic baths in Budapest, patients and tourists alike partaking of thermal baths, steam rooms, saunas and swimming.

Scott parked on the street and, as Rachel got out, she said, "I'll take the back," handed him the tracking palm pilot, and headed toward an alley that would take her behind the looming, ornate structure.

"Rachel!" Scott said.

She paused and looked back.

"Be careful," he said.

"You too," she said, and took off.

"For shit's sake," Robinson said. "Are you two gonna turn sappy, all of a sudden? You're spies, remember? Deadly spies!"

"Keep it in mind," Scott said.

They were up the stairs and at the doors when Robinson turned to Scott and said, rather wistfully, "You realize there's a good chance I can make two kinds of history today?"

"How so?"

"I can help save the world, *and* make the boxing record books."

"I like to see you staying positive like this."

Soon they were entering the spa, a magnificent chamber with an arched stained-glass ceiling whose yellow and gold panes gave the cathedral-like space a warm glow. At left and right, under pillars sporting fern-adorned rather mediterranean-looking balconies, were areas with benches; between was a vast swimming pool, bluer than the Danube.

"Like swimmin' in church," Robinson said under his breath.

And before the two fully clothed spies, scattered about the large hot pool, were naked men, ranging in age from mid-twenties to late sixties.

Several of the unadorned bathers, carrying but not covered by towels, looked at the two dressed intruders, frowning.

Flashing his grin, not quite hiding his discomfort, Robinson nodded to these men, saying, "Hey there . . . how you hangin'? . . . Nice to see ya. . . ."

Although, in reality, the champ was studiously avoiding seeing much of anything. . . .

That grin frozen, Robinson whispered, "Okay, Scotty . . . what kind of gay bathhouse shit you get me into?"

Ignoring this, Scott checked the tracking device. "Gundars is here—back there. In the sauna, I think."

Heading to the left, weaving through benches where naked men sat in the steamy pool room, resting, chatting, the secret agent led the fighter toward the rear of the chamber. About halfway there Scott paused, glancing at Robinson, beside him.

"We just lost the signal," Scott said.

"Maybe the walls is just too thick around here."

"I don't think so. . . . I was getting a strong signal before . . . then it was as if somebody shut off the bug."

"Or stepped on it. S'what you do with bugs."

Nodding, Scott glanced around. "Something's wrong. We need to abort."

As Scott turned and began heading back the way they'd come, Robinson stopped him with a hand on the arm. "Whoa, whoa, whoa—we're *havin'* this baby."

Scott frowned. "What?"

"We ain't walkin' away. You wanna deny a brother his parade? Which means we gotta go back there and get that plane."

"You actually think the plane is here?"

"Hell yeah—it's stashed back in that sauna, man."

Scott sighed. "A forty-ton airplane . . . stuffed into a sauna?"

"You ask, how could they do that? But I say, we'll find out how, when we bust these mothers. . . . Hell, maybe they broke the puppy down into parts. Chop shop-style."

"Something else your uncle taught you?"

"Not that my uncle would know a thing about that kinda shit."

"Kel, come on . . . we're outta here."

"Hold up. . . ." Robinson stood with his legs apart. "I'm gettin' somethin'. . . ."

Scott closed his eyes, shook his head. "Please tell me your 'boys' aren't talking to you."

"Some kinds of trackin' shit don't show up on your damn screen. . . . Oh yeah. Definitely a plane in there. Boys are buzzin' like a chainsaw."

"Kel . . ."

Robinson's brow tightened. "You tellin' me a good agent don't listen to his instincts? That when you're in the field, you don't listen to your gut? Well, I get my signals a little lower down, is all."

And the champ headed back toward the door to a room labeled STEAM and MASSAGE (in several languages, English included). Against his better judgment, Alexander Scott followed his friend's lead.

They passed through double doors into a cavernous space draped with steam, and if their clothes had clung to them before, now the two spies were draped in the dampness of immediate, heavy perspiration. Built-into-the-floor tile benches were all around, and perhaps a dozen men—the youngest in his late fifties—were naked but for white diaper-like pants; and the old men were flogging each other with tree branches, to release sweat, and increase circulation.

Taking this bizarre sight in, Robinson said to his partner, "No offense, man, but white people sure do some crazy-ass shit, sometimes."

"No argument," Scott said, trying to see through the haze.

The men began rising and—taking their branches and diapers with them, sometimes singly, sometimes in pairs—exited. This made Scott frown: the sauna dwellers had seen the two fully clothed men enter, and shortly after began to file out . . . had they been told, beforehand, to do so?

"Uh oh," Scott said.

"What?"

"Not good."

"Try to be more vague . . . otherwise I might understand."

"Let's just say *my* boys are tingling. . . ."

Scott took stock: four men remained, and they were not elderly. This quartet was positioned around the room, covering pretty much the entire space, naked men seated with large towels over their midsection. Even if, as Robinson had speculated, this *was* a gay bath, Scott couldn't justify the size of the bulges beneath those towels. . . .

He threw himself at Robinson, tackling the champ, pushing him behind the largest of the built-in tile benches. Almost simultaneously, the four stragglers threw off their towels to reveal bathing suits . . . and UZIs.

The machine-gun chatter echoed through the tiled room like an awful, dissonant choir, perfect for this cathedral setting. Bullets shattered tiles, carved notches in the stone walls, and paid special attention to the bench the spies huddled down behind, decimating the other side of it.

"Why the hell are naked guys shooting at us?" Robinson asked, hands over his head, eyes wide and wild.

"They're in bathing suits, actually."

"Oh, yeah, well that's a whole different deal! What the hell's up with this shit?"

"It's an ambush."

"You think?"

Scott had his small glock in hand now, and he risked a peek over the bench, just enough time to fix the position of two of the shooters as being directly opposite them; the other two were off to the right, at various points. He ducked down a fraction of a second before the top of the bench shattered under the thunder of UZI, the brittle rain of expended shell casings accompanying it.

Robinson looked at Scott with desperation in his eyes. "Their guns are bigger than yours."

"This whole size thing is a myth."

"You wish—you got a sure way out, right?"

". . . Not this time."

The UZI fire was chipping and chopping away at the bench, dust and slivers flying.

"Not this time?" Robinson said. "Not this time! I thought that was a *rule,* man!"

"Well, it's not so much a rule as a guideline."

A lessening of fire indicated at least one of them was reloading; Scott leaned around the side and threw a couple slugs their way, then ducked back.

"You said 'rule,' " Robinson insisted.

"More, a goal."

"I definitely heard 'rule!' "

The gunfire hammered away at them.

"Scotty, how many bullets you got left in that little squirt gun?"

"Six."

Scott, down low, almost prone, looked up: the ceiling was a nest of pipes, stretching across the length of the room. Aiming carefully, the spy shot one of the pipes; water began to stream down. Then he shot another: same effect.

Sounding mildly hysterical, Robinson said, "Hate to second-guess a pro, Scotty, but if we only got six bullets left . . . *four,* now . . . maybe we should shoot at the bad guys—the ones shootin' at us? You can always kill the ceiling, later."

Scott fired again, hitting a third pipe; but this time water did not stream. Instead, they could hear the hiss of escaping gas.

"There we go," Scott said, all but drowned out by the UZI fire.

"You wouldn't care to let me in on what you're up to? Or would that spoil the damn surprise?"

As UZIs chattered at them, Scott—from the shot-up portion of the bench—loosened and then removed a brick, which he handed to Kel.

"What do I do with this, Scotty? Hit myself as hard in the head with it as I can?"

"Toss it up next to the hole in that pipe . . . the hissing one. We need a spark."

Getting it, Robinson said, "Hard to get much leverage, crouched down like this. . . ."

Assuming a squashed version of a shooter's stance, Scott said, "You can do it, man. . . ."

Robinson tossed the brick.

Scott fired, hitting the object at the apex of its rise.

Nothing—just the clunk of the brick coming back down to earth.

UZI fire taunted them as they ducked way back down, Scott saying, "That wasn't an ideal toss."

"These ain't exactly ideal conditions. For brick tossing."

Scott acquired another brick, held it out to Robinson. "Focus. Concentrate. Stay positive."

"Please don't say . . ."

"Be the brick."

"Damn."

Scott took aim, saying, casually, "By the way, this is our last bullet."

"That's not helping me stay positive," Robinson said.

And, as more gunfire rattled the room, the champ hefted the brick, lofting that sucker, and Scott squeezed the trigger. . . .

The bullet hit the brick, all right, sparking, igniting the gas spewing from the punctured pipe. At first the result seemed small—the pipe exploded at each gate valve, but nothing damaging enough to effect the current standoff.

But Alexander Scott knew that the pipe would lead to a large gas heater—necessary to heat these baths— and the chain reaction would be inexorable. Once the fireball that was surely streaking down the pipe reached that tank, the resulting explosion should create a nice diversion. . . .

It created much more than that.

The explosion was huge, the fireball enormous now, rocking the entire venerable structure, the blast ripping through the room, hurling the two shooters opposite them into the air like discarded beer bottles, the UZIs flung to the floor, where the weapons plopped into the water provided by the other overhead pipes Scott had pierced.

In the meantime, Scott and Robinson kissed the floor, protected behind the bench.

When the flames had receded, Scott said, "Go!"

The two men emerged from either side of the bench to splash across the floor to those fallen UZIs, sliding through the wetness to the guns. Then Robinson had one of the weapons, and Scott the other, and they turned toward the other end of the room, where the other two shooters lurked behind their own benches, one of them disoriented by the blast enough to be caught offguard.

A burst from Scott's UZI dropped him to splash in more than just water, but the final man in trunks made a break for the rear door.

Robinson let loose with the UZI and carved up the wall and much of the door and door frame, but the final shooter slipped out in time to avoid everything except the noise.

About to pursue the bastard, Robinson felt Scott's hand on his arm.

"Forget him!" Scott yelled. "We've got to get to Rachel!"

Robinson nodded, saying, "Ambush means they knew we were comin', means she's in trouble, too!"

"Any way you slice it, Kel, they'll be after her!"

They were both running now, heading back the way they came, rushing out through the cathedral-like spa, when suddenly Scott veered toward a set of French doors.

"This way!" he said.

They emerged onto a veranda outside the baths and above the alley; from here they could see an Audi, speeding away, tires squealing, the vehicle heading for the Szabadsag Bridge.

"There she is!" Robinson said, pointing.

From their perch they could see the lovely secret agent down there, on the street below, running for their parked car.

"Rachel!" Scott called.

She glanced back, smiled ferally, yelling, "I got him!"

They watched as she ran to the car, saw her get in and start it up.

Robinson gripped Scott's arm. "Man, they knew we were here! You gotta stop her!"

"Rach! *Stop!*"

But the beautiful agent had already put the car in gear; the clunky little vehicle took off, and followed the fleeing Audi onto the bridge.

She made it perhaps one hundred feet before the car exploded into a demonic rising fireball not unlike the one that minutes before had bailed Scott and Robinson out of their trouble.

And, for that matter, all of her troubles would be over now, too.

10

Black smoke, with spirals of gray, plumed into a pale blue sky, up through the bridge suspension cables, the deeper blue of the Danube providing an eerily peaceful contrast.

Kelly Robinson glanced at his friend, the boxer already sick over the tragic implications this held for the low-key secret agent. Scott gripped the edge of the balcony on the spa terrace; the two spies were frozen there, in slack-jawed horror. Shrill alarms, set off by the blast, drilled at the stillness of the afternoon, punctuated by the shouts and cries of pedestrians and other drivers; and within seconds distant screams of sirens began their inevitable increase of volume.

And the clunky little car, where the beautiful Rachel Wright had sat, was mute witness to it all—a charred, smoldering snarl of steel.

Robinson hated to ask, but he was the apprentice here; he had no choice. "Alex . . . Scotty—what do we do?"

Scott turned toward the champ, who was startled by the stony, stoic expression on the surfer-boy countenance.

"We go," Scott said.

And the agent headed back inside, neither hurrying nor tarrying.

Robinson, sick to his stomach, glanced at the charcoal smoke, coiling into the sky. "Scotty. . . . We can't just leave. Don't we go after the bad guys? Should we talk to the cops? What . . . ?"

Coldly, Scott said, "I told you at the start of this—it's a black op. Black enough for you yet?"

The sarcasm twisted in Robinson like a knife; he liked this man, and he knew Scotty had just suffered a horrible loss. . . . He would cut him as much slack as he could.

"We have to do something, Alex."

"We don't exist."

And Scott went back inside the spa.

Robinson hustled after him; when Scott tossed his UZI to the floor, like a discarded paper cup, the boxer followed suit. Nothing was said between them for perhaps five minutes, as they took backstreets of Budapest, on foot, heading back toward the BNS warehouse. Scott was walking quickly, so much so that this fittest-of-the-fit athlete could hardly keep pace.

"Yo, Alex—hold up."

But Scott kept on walking. Fast.

Robinson fell in alongside him, as they moved along sparsely populated sidewalks in a residential section of multi-story eighteenth century homes, each painted a different pastel, providing a quaint unreality to the aftermath of the tragedy.

"Look, man," Robinson said, easily, "it's messed up, but don't these things happen? Wasn't our fault, Gundars was on to us. We're spies. Bad shit happens to good people."

Scott stopped so abruptly, Robinson almost lost his balance, stopping, too.

"Excuse me," Scott said, the coldness a virtual chill now, "did you just call yourself a spy?"

Hurt, Robinson said, "You *made* me a spy, man—I was content not to be. I did already have another job, you know."

"*I* am a spy," Scott said, acidly, pointing to himself. "*Rachel Wright* was a spy. You are a civilian, and a means to an end. Don't flatter yourself."

Shaking his head, Robinson said, "Scotty, please . . . I know you're upset . . . and she was a good woman . . ."

Scott pointed a finger at him, like a gun. "You're right—she was. Past tense. And yet you're still here— the 'spy' who listens to his dick, the boxer whose instincts are in his boxers."

"Please, Scotty—I know you're hurting, man. But don't go there."

"Where?"

Robinson shook his head, woefully. "Layin' the blame on me, what happened."

Scott's smile was a terrible thing. "Oh no, never. Of course not. Your fault? Who could blame you? Just because I said abort and you insisted on having your 'baby.' You're the King of the Universe. You just wanted your parade. Only now it's a funeral march."

The fighter held up two open palms. "Okay, man, you're steppin' over the line. You need to back this shit off."

Scott perked an ear, lowering his head. "That can't be you talking—that must be your 'boys.' Those genius gonads . . ."

"That's it," Robinson said, fed up. "No more."

Scott snorted a laugh. "Or what?"

The fighter shoved the secret agent—not hard. Just enough to make a point. They were at the mouth of an alley, and the conversation made its way off the street, a ways, into the relative privacy of facing walls and garbage cans.

"What?" Scott said, apparently amused. "You want to fight?"

"No." Robinson shook his head. "Just want this shit to stop."

"Maybe we *should* go a few rounds—might be fun. You might find out the difference between a civilian and a pro."

"I am a pro," Robinson said humorlessly. "These are lethal weapons, man. Don't screw with me."

Scott started circling him, hands assuming the blade-like form of the martial artist. "You've been trained to fight in a little square 'ring'—I've been trained to kill a man, anywhere . . . anytime. Want some, Champ?"

Circling too, fists up, Robinson said, "Don't do this, Alex . . ."

"Come on—it'll be amusing."

"If you think two weeks of dental work's amusing, yeah."

"Fair warning," Scott said, and he held up a thumb and forefinger. "I could kill you with these two fingers."

And the world middleweight champion threw a punch, lightning fast, connecting solidly with Scott's face, smashing the oft-broken nose yet again. The secret agent's head snapped back, his knees buckling.

"Thanks for the warning," Robinson said, fists up, his expression intense—no bullshit.

Scott assumed a full fighting posture—martial arts-style, nothing comical about it: Jet Li or Jackie Chan would have looked at the spy and known they had a serious challenger. . . .

But Robinson, falling into his trademark, cocky, dancing style, mocked his opponent: "Well, well, well . . . check out the surfer boy, tryin' to be all ninja and shit."

Scott spun, delivering a high, roundhouse kick, which Robinson ducked beneath; but when the boxer came back up, the spy's other foot was waiting to crush Robinson's solar plexus with a powerful front kick.

The champ, doubling over, staggered back.

"That just knocked the wind out of you," Scott said lightly, not at all winded himself. "Two inches, you'd be dead. Heart stopped. Had enough?"

Catching his breath—and it wasn't easy—Kelly Robinson straightened up, gathered his dignity, and said, "Why didn't you say you was gonna kick like a girl? I didn't expect that sissy shit outa you, Scotty . . . but now that I know what rules we're playin' by . . ."

And Robinson abandoned his ring training for his street savvy, slamming a kick into Scott's balls, unmercifully hard.

Scott doubled over, in obvious, excruciating pain.

"Now your boys are talkin' to *you*," Robinson said, and came in, throwing a vicious right hand.

But Scott slipped the punch, caught the arm, twisted it, then kicked the fighter's legs out from under him, sending him flipping onto the windshield of a parked car, the glass cracking a thousand times, spiderwebbing under the impact.

Scott came down with an elbow, but Robinson rolled away just in time, the elbow decimating the windshield, as the boxer jumped down off the car.

Now, deadly serious, they faced off, circling, no longer in the alley, out on the sidewalk, in the sunshine.

A small crowd had gathered in the quiet neighborhood, across the street and on either side of them. Both men knew they should not be attracting this kind of attention, but they had each, in the heat of battle, boiled down to their essence: boxer facing killer.

The bystanders then witnessed something every one of them would remember to the ends of their days, and yet would never do the event justice, in the retelling.

The two warriors went at each other with everything in their individual arsenals—fists flying, feet whirling, magnificent martial art moves, scientific boxing strategies, in a flurry of action that revealed the incredible skill of each fighting man . . .

. . . and yet neither landed more than a fleeting, glancing blow on the other.

Perhaps one would have killed the other; perhaps both would have died before the emotionally-charged duel came to a natural conclusion. But no one would ever know, as a Hungarian police car rolled in, pulling up in the street; two cops, a tall one and squat one, both with guns in hand, leapt out and rushed the pair.

The tall cop said, in Hungarian, "What's going on here?"

The two men froze, and Robinson had no idea what had just been said, though the gist wasn't hard to imagine.

Scott, however, fluent speaker of the language that he was, replied in the local tongue: "This black man tried to mug me."

And the two cops with guns closed in on Kelly Robinson, who raised his hands and grinned nervously, saying, "Yo! What are you nice men doin' pointin' those things at me?"

Then they were dragging him from the scene, shoving him into the squad car, ignoring his indignant cries, including a pitiful repetition of, "Don't you know who I am? I'm Kelly Robinson!"

Apparently they didn't.

One of the cops gave Scott a card, saying in Hungarian, "Can you come to the stationhouse, under your own steam? We'll need you to sign a complaint, to make a statement."

"I'll be right down," Scott said, with a glazed smile.

And then the cops, and Kelly Robinson, were gone.

Alexander Scott leaned against the alley wall and,

finally, the crowd dispersed. When he was alone, Scott entered the alley, and sat between two garbage cans, and for a short time, he covered his face and wept.

But only for a short time.

When the spy returned to the warehouse that shielded the "secret" BNS headquarters, he discovered that their secret was out . . .

. . . the location was a shambles, the banks of equipment destroyed, as if by baseball bats or maybe tire irons, smashed to pieces. This was pretty much par for the course, in the spy game, and no great tragedy.

Less easily written off were the two techs on the cement floor—Jim and Bob—both of whom had been shot to death, wearing the red stitching that suggested extinction by UZI.

"My God," Scott said, after checking the bodies.

The mission was a disaster . . . a debacle . . . the worst botch of his career. . . .

A phone began to ring.

On one of the counters arrayed with destroyed equipment, the only item the invaders hadn't demolished—perhaps it had been too low-tech for them to bother with—was that single telephone.

What the hell—Scott answered it.

"Yeah," he said numbly.

"What in God's name is going on there?" McIntyre's voice demanded.

Scott was not surprised to hear his superior's voice; Mac was just about the only person on the planet who had this number—living person, at least.

"I've been calling for hours," Mac's voice said, the frustration, the concern, palpable.

"Um . . . we hit a few snags," Scott said, eyes unavoidably taking in the death and destruction all around him.

"How bad?"

"You're talking to the sole survivor."

". . . my God. Rachel too?"

"You should be getting word, soon. Car explosion. Szabadsag Bridge."

"What about Robinson?"

"I took him out."

"What do you mean, took him out?"

"He's alive, but I removed him from the picture. He's sidetracked right now, and then he'll be caught up in his own life. His fight's in a few hours."

"I see. Alex, you do understand: we can't abort. The Switchblade is—"

"I'll recover it. It's here. I'll find it."

"Alex, a positive attitude won't be enough . . ."

Scott's mouth performed something that was technically a smile—his lips pulled back over his teeth; but describing it as a smile would have been inaccurate, somehow.

He said to his chief, "I wouldn't call my attitude, right now, positive, exactly . . . but I am positive I'll recover your goddamn plane."

A pause indicated Mac was trying to read his agent's state of mind; then the voice over the phone said: "I'm sending back-up."

"No. There's no time—I have to get back to that palace."

"Under what guise?"

"Under no guise. The clock is ticking—that plane will be in terrorist hands in a matter of hours . . . maybe minutes. There's a computer in Gundars's study that can tell me right where that plane is sitting."

"Then you don't know where it is, yet?"

"Mac, sorry. I gotta go."

And he hung up on his boss.

Scott went to a hidden supply closest, and fortunately that seemed to be one secret that hadn't been spilled: the agent was able to outfit himself with an UZI of his own. He helped himself to a shoulder strap and three extra clips.

Then he set out to find the Switchblade. He didn't know how much Gundars would get for it, from his terrorist high bidder; but he did know the price tag was high . . . including as it did the lives of three BNS agents.

The American Embassy vouched for Kelly Robinson; he spent less than an hour at the Hungarian police stationhouse—which was as dreary a place as he might have imagined—and when he arrived, by apologetic police escort, at the Budapest sports arena, the fight was less than half an hour away. The arena—in the promenade area shared by various luxury hotels, and with a postcard view of Castle Hill across the Danube, the Chain Bridge nearby—was swarming with fight fans, many of whom recognized him, pointing, calling to him.

But for once he did not preen, or mug, refusing autographs politely but firmly.

When he finally wandered into the locker room, he found his posse—T.J., Darryl and Jerry, who had not seen him since he stormed out of the tiny basement room at the hotel, a hundred years ago . . . that is, last night. They were milling about, anxious as hell, sick with worry.

His massive bodyguard, the bald goateed Jerry, brightened like Christmas at the sight of the champ, but then immediately darkened, a parent thrilled to see his delinquent kid turn up, and at the same time furious with him.

"Where the hell you been, Kel?" Jerry demanded, gesturing with open, finger-splayed hands, like a basketball player who desperately wanted to be passed the ball. "You fight in twenty damn minutes!"

"Can't you tell?" wiry T.J. said, grinning, thrilled to see the champ, who looked haggard, his clothes ragged, signs of the street brawl on his face. "He finally messed with the wrong dude's woman! What's up, Champ? Some local boy write his address on your ass?"

Robinson went to his locker, wordlessly. "I gotta get dressed."

"Where's the white boy?" bald, bouncy Darryl said. "Thought he was your assistant, now—must not've made much of a bodyguard."

"He's not on the team anymore," Robinson said

coldly. He turned a hard gaze on his crew. "You through busting my chops? Or can we get ready for this fight?"

And the bullshit stopped, and Robinson and his posse got down with it.

In a taxi, barely a block away, the champ's former assistant—hoping to get across the Chain Bridge, for a return visit to the palace where Arnold Gundars regularly held court—was stuck bumper-to-bumper in traffic. At his side was a duffel bag with an UZI in it; his stomach was tight, the urgency—and an unadmitted thirst for revenge—was a white-hot reality under a coolly professional surface.

"This traffic . . . is fault of the boxer fight," the cabby said, apologetically, speaking his broken English, even though his American passenger had hired him in Hungarian.

From the backseat, Scott could see the looming sports arena, the swirling klieg lights, the flapping banners, sidewalks filled with swarming fans. Even now, Kelly Robinson was a pain in the ass, screwing up the mission.

Fed up, Scott thrust a handful of paper money at the driver, and got out of the cab, hauling his duffel bag.

Moving through the sportsfans on the sidewalks, who were heading in the opposite direction, the secret agent—just another tourist in a black sportcoat and dark blue shirt, apparently harmless—made his way toward the oldest, arguably the most beautiful of Budapest's seven spans over the Danube. The Nazis had destroyed it, but the Chain Bridge had been rebuilt, post-war, slightly widened for traffic, and was as good a symbol as any of Budapest's resiliency in a world where evil persisted.

Running past the backed-up traffic, toward the bridge's pedestrian walkway, Scott noticed the sports arena's spotlight beam swinging around, and catching the graceful lines of the symmetrical suspension bridge, including the heavy arch-like turrets of the structure.

It was as if Kelly Robinson were lighting the way for Alexander Scott, and—for the first time since their street fight—the decent man that Scott was, despite the dirty job he did, reared up within him . . . and he felt a pang of guilt, over the way he had treated this man, who had in fact become his friend . . . the cocky civilian who had offered his help to Uncle Sam, and who had risked his life for his "bro," Scotty. . . .

If he lived through this, Alex Scott promised himself he would apologize to Kel . . . who deserved better than getting Scott's emotional garbage tossed in his face, like that.

He'd called Kel a prick; but Scott knew he was the one who'd behaved badly, this afternoon . . . he'd been the prick, the arrogant asshole . . . not Kelly Robinson.

And it was at that moment, as the secret agent realized a personal failing even as he pushed through the fight fans toward the legendary Chain Bridge, that Alexander Scott spotted the Switchblade.

Thanks to the sports arena's swinging klieg light, the nearest of the bridge turrets had been illuminated, revealing several pigeons perched there . . .

. . . in mid-air.

The pigeons seemed to be sitting on air, about ten feet above the turret. Another pigeon, and another pigeon, alighted there, on nothing at all.

But Alex Scott knew that they were, in reality, sitting on an invisible airplane.

And for the first time since Rachel's death, Alexander Scott grinned.

"Gotcha," he said.

Thinking, *Thanks, Kel,* he ran toward the bridge.

11

....

From the perspective of Kelly Robinson's corner, there was little way to tell that this blur of bright lights in the darkness was not an arena in the United States—and indeed the packed, enthusiastic house was made up of boxing fans not only from Hungary but from all over Europe and, yes, the U.S., too. As he danced and bobbed and loosened up, Robinson slowly scanned the crowd, most of whom were reacting to his antics with the usual crazed gusto.

In the front row, however, to the right of his corner, sat three large, very somber-looking men, who watched him coldly; Robinson had a strong suspicion the trio—dressed in dark suits and ties, shaved apes all spruced up for a night on the town—could not have cared less about the championship fight about to go down.

More than a suspicion, actually: he recognized two of three from the party at the palace last night—members of Arnold Gundars's security force.

Of course, it wasn't unnatural that they would be here, or that they'd have such good seats. After all, Gundars owned Cedric Mills, or the fighter's contract, anyway. Curiously, at the coveted ringside seats, there was no sign of Gundars himself. . . .

"Yo, Darryl," Robinson said, dancing lightly, studying the brawny trio.

The bald corner man was there in a flash. "Yo, Kel."

"See those three dudes, first row?"

"I see 'em. If they was any uglier, my eyes'd bleed."

"That's them . . . I don't want 'em near me. Understood? Ever."

"You got it, boss."

"And when the fight's over, 'specially . . . watch the suckers."

"Like a hawk, Kel."

Darryl, walking along the outer ring, clued T.J. in.

T.J. said, "So the white boy's out and you're in, I see."

"I'm back, baby." He high-fived T.J. "We're *all* back."

"Best of all, Kel's back. . . . He'll knock this Slavic sucker into last week."

"Hey . . . check this out. . . ."

Some very foxy-looking, scantily attired ring girls were circling; they held up cards reading: ROUND ONE. And, in so doing, revealed tufts of hair under their arms.

"Damn!" T.J. said, wincing. "What the hell is wrong with these foreign bitches!"

"It's the pits," Darryl said, making a face.

The opening bell sounded, and Robinson in (appropriately) kelly-green trunks emerged from his corner, and sour-looking Cedric Mills, in trunks as blue as the Danube, came out from his.

As a ring announcer was saying, "*And here we go*," Mills bore right in on the champ and unceremoniously threw a punch that caught Robinson on the side of the face, sending him stumbling back into his corner.

At ringside, over the screams of fans, one of the announcers was saying, "*Wow! The European champ means business! Not giving the American champ any chance to find his groove. . . .*"

The other announcer said, "*Maybe two fights in one week wasn't such a great idea, after all, Bob.*"

In Robinson's corner, his crew called out to him, Jerry the loudest, saying, "Wake up out there, damnit!"

"Shut up, Jerry," Robinson said, waiting.

When Mills came in for a follow-up, Robinson slipped the punch, and responded with two solid body blows, visibly rocking Mills, the crowd roaring. The challenger backed off, his small victory over.

The fight would start now.

His white hair riffling in the wind, Arnold Gundars— looking solemn yet dapper in a dark blue suit, lighter blue shirt and dark blue tie—was conducting a business meeting atop one of the arched turrets of the Chain Bridge.

The night was dark, but the bridge itself was well-lighted, the twin turrets themselves fully illuminated as were the suspension supports, in a fashion that from a distance recalled strings of white Christmas lights. Traffic below was steady, and Gundars rather relished the nature of the exchange. How much more out in the open could an illegal transaction be?

The top of the turret was a rectangular deck, with shoulder-high walls, so it was doubtful anyone below could see Gundars, his assorted thugs or their guests, General Zhu Tam and his several bodyguards, and his pilot, all out of uniform tonight. For a business affair, the dress was casual—dark jackets, dark trousers, the occasional handgun . . . one must not be *overly* trustworthy, when dealing with the likes of Zhu Tam.

Or, for that matter, Arnold Gundars.

At the edge of the platform-like turret rooftop, the Switchblade perched in all its invisible glory, though at such close range, its sleek outline could just be made out, enough so, at least, that Zhu Tam could admire the costly piece of hardware he was buying.

Gundars watched with satisfaction as Zhu Tam said something in Korean to one of his flunkies, sending the man ducking under the fuselage; coming up on the other side, the flunky turned and faced the plane, and his image appeared on the fuselage in front of Zhu Tam . . . as if the general could see right through the jet. The illusion was perfection, technology at its most magical.

Zhu Tam touched the ship—he knew it was there, and his fingertips confirmed as much—and his eyes opened wide, in child-like wonder.

"Mr. Gundars," the general said, "this is the most incredible thing I have ever seen."

"Or not," Gundars said, glibly.

The general turned to his host, smiling, nodding.

No one on the turret top noticed the perching pigeons that had given them all away.

*   *   *

The suspension cable was wider than one might imagine, and—for maintenance purposes—handrails made passage safe . . . relatively so. On the other hand, Alexander Scott was running up the steep, seemingly endless slope, in the dark, an UZI on a strap slung under his sportcoat. The wind whipped at his jacket and hair, just cold enough, crisp enough, to help him stay alert.

Finally he reached the ledge—the top of the turret was the equivalent, perhaps, of five or six stories above him—where a door awaited.

The secret agent slipped inside, into a stairwell guarded by one of Gundars's guards, a bearded brute in a dark jacket, his own UZI in his hands.

That UZI snapped to attention, trained on Scott; but the spy put his hands up and approached gingerly.

"It's okay," Scott said in Hungarian. He had car keys in his hands—to his Jag at home, actually—and he shook them, as if trying to get the attention of a kid. "Mr. Gundars sent for me—forgot the keys to the plane. I got them right here."

The guard took this in with a confused expression, mixed with skepticism; but Scott was close enough now to chop the heel of his hand into the guard's trachea.

The man was dead before he dropped, but he did drop.

And Scott headed up the steps.

At the sports arena, the fight was going well for Kelly Robinson, who had left behind, before stepping into this ring, any and all thought of his brief excursion into the world of secret agents.

Now he had his groove, all right—one beautiful combination after another either hurting or befuddling his outclassed challenger.

Robinson paused between blows to ask, "Say, Ced— which side you want the swellin' on . . . left or right?"

Furious, Mills swung, and Robinson ducked.

Dancing, the champ said, "You're gonna leave it up to me, then? Ced, you are one gracious damn host. . . . All right, we'll go center."

The next punch went right down the middle, snapping back his opponent's head.

Robinson, playing, in complete command, put on a mock-sympathetic face. "Oooh, Ced—that had to hurt. You know what you need? You need a nap. . . ."

And before Mills could recover from the last punishing blow, Robinson landed a huge punch to the head that staggered the man.

The ring announcers confirmed the obvious: *"Bob, I have to say Robinson is dominating this fight."*

"Mills is definitely taking a lot of punishment out there, but he is game, all right . . . and in top shape. Doesn't look any the worse for wear, despite all the champ has leveled at him."

"Maybe so, Bob, but let's see how Cedric looks after ten more rounds of Kelly Robinson."

His legs rubbery, Mills tried to come back at the champ with an uppercut, but Robinson ducked it easily, countering with several quick hard punches.

Kelly Robinson may have been in Hungary, but he

was nonetheless home. Dancing around, he grinned and reached into his usual bag of psychological-warfare tricks.

"Yo, Ced—lemme ask you somethin', man—you got a girl here? Where's she sittin'?"

And as Mills thought that one over, Robinson slammed another huge right into the challenger's mid-section.

Alexander Scott, at the top of the stairs, slowly cracked the door, peeking out onto the turret roof, where all of his suspicions were confirmed.

The vaguest outline of the Switchblade could be seen, at the turret's far edge; and, not vague at all, five pigeons sat on the "invisible" plane.

Quite visible was Arnold Gundars, attended by assorted goons. The arms dealer was watching as General Zhu Tam tapped a few keys on a laptop computer inside an open briefcase, using a knee-high vent shaft as a makeshift table. A digital red line shot across the laptop's screen.

" 'Transaction complete,' " the general said, reading from the screen.

"The two sweetest words in the English language," Gundars said.

Gundars looked to his own man, a few feet away at another vent with another laptop; a nod of confirmation put a smile on Gundars's face.

"Congratulations, General," Gundars said. "You are now the proud owner of the most advanced piece of weaponry on the planet."

The two men—arms dealer and general—approached each other and shook hands, nodding, smiling.

Gundars reached inside his jacket pocket and withdrew a small sheet of paper.

"And this insignificant, harmless series of numbers," Gundars said, handing the paper toward the general, "seals the final act of our transaction . . . the ignition code."

Scott's eyes tightened. *Good,* he thought. *Good.* . . .

Zhu Tam took the paper, but Gundars didn't let go, saying, in his pixie-ish way, "A small favor, General?"

"Anything, my friend."

"I travel quite a lot, so I would appreciate the courtesy of a 'heads up' before you annihilate any particular city. . . . You needn't tell me which, as long as it's not the city I'm in. Wouldn't want to compromise a military effort. . . . Just let me know if I might need to, well, temporarily restrict my travel plans."

"No problem," the general said, genially. "We would not want to lose such a valuable friend."

"Or supplier," Gundars said, with a mischievous smile.

And he released the paper.

The general called his pilot over and handed the ignition code to him. This routine piece of business seized the attention of Gundars and his men enough for Scott to slip onto the turret deck, the UZI out from under his jacket. He crept up, eased behind Gundars and pressed the small deadly snout of the weapon to the back of the arms dealer's neck—a cold-metal kiss that made Gundars jump a little, in surprise . . . and recognition.

"That was rude," Scott said. "You guys starting without me."

The Gundars goons swiveled around, as did the Korean general's bodyguards, and all of them tried to see, to decide, if they had a good shot at the intruder.

They did not.

"Since your watchdogs might not listen to me," Scott said to Gundars, in English, the UZI's nose still in the nape of the man's neck, "this would be a good time for you to tell them to put down their weapons."

Gundars nodded to his men, who grudgingly complied.

"Don't drop the guns—they might go off," Scott said in Hungarian. "Just set them down, soft, slow."

The goons did so.

"And, General," Scott said in Korean, "would you be so kind as to likewise instruct your men, as well?"

Zhu Tam nodded curtly, then, in that language, told his men to lay down their arms.

"Arnold," Scott said affably, "did you *really* think you could roll over the BNS like that?"

But now a cold kiss of metal touched Scott . . . specifically his left temple—the tip of an automatic handgun.

And an all-too familiar voice said, "Actually, that's exactly what we thought . . . Alex."

The lovely voice, especially the way she rolled the "l" in his name, was something he never thought he'd be lucky enough to enjoy again, this side of heaven; and wasn't this a hell of a way to hear it.

He glimpsed Rachel Wright's beautiful, ruthless features, just barely, before she raised the automatic and brought down the grip to slam into the back of his head.

He'd fallen for her a long time ago—for her beauty, and—it would seem—her act; now he fell again.

When he came around, Alexander Scott found himself at Rachel Wright's feet. There had been a time—earlier today, in fact—when he would have been glad to find himself in this position; but things had changed, even though she was still just as beautiful in her *Avengers*-style black-leather togs.

The secret agent didn't know how long he'd been out—probably only a minute or so; but everyone's position on the turret deck had shifted somewhat, notably that of the pilot, who now sat in the Switchblade's cockpit, ready to start up the plane. Only the head and shoulders of the Korean pilot were visible, and this would not be the case once the cockpit canopy slid into place.

The pigeons were gone, apparently spooked by the pilot.

"Hands behind your head," Rachel said.

He complied, saying, "Gotta hand it to you, Rach . . . pretty convincing, that whole tragic death deal."

She shrugged, her mouth a thin cruel line . . . thin

beautiful cruel line. "You pick up a trick or two, over the years."

"Rolled out before it blew?"

"Under that nearby bus, yes. . . . You really should have caught it."

"I was distracted."

"Distracted, Alex?"

"By the sound of my *heart breaking*."

He thought he saw something human flicker in her eyes, but then she said, "In this heartless business? If so, you should never have got into the game, you sweet silly fool."

He put as much contempt into his smile as he could muster. "See, Rach? I knew you cared."

A blaring alarm made everyone jump . . . everyone but Scott. The shrill bleating emerged from the space where the Switchblade sat, its form barely detectable. The cockpit canopy slid back, revealing the upper part of the confused, concerned pilot, a partial head-and-shoulders torso floating above the turret deck.

Then a crackling sound accompanied a flickering into view of the sleek, gray-blue needle-nosed jet; the image shimmered there, then winked out again, leaving only that floating partial pilot to stare back, stunned and perhaps afraid.

"Ooooh," Scott said, looking up at Rachel in mock concern, "that can't be good. . . . Of course it's just a prototype. I'm sure the general and his crack Korean scientists'll work out the bugs."

Confusion spread like a rash across the rooftop group. "Watch him," Rachel said to a burly, bearded

Gundars guard. "He's much more dangerous than he looks."

Scott beamed at her. "Why, thanks, Rach—that means a lot."

Gundars and Zhu Tam were exchanging concerned, vaguely accusatory looks. The arms dealer approached the floating half-pilot.

"What the hell did you do?" Gundars demanded of the man.

But the general defended the flier. "He is our best pilot—show respect!"

The partial man in the cockpit held up the piece of paper that Gundars had provided. In English, the man said, "I enter ignition code. That is all I do."

Scott watched, rather enjoying the surrealistic sight, as Rachel—like a blind woman, but a skillful one—felt along the side of the invisible plane; when she had located the wing, she hopped up, with acrobatic grace, seeming to be kneeling in mid-air, as she gazed in at the cockpit. In black leather, her behind, as she crouched, looked lovely; unfortunately, it was probably the nicest thing about her, now.

Scott knew what she would be seeing: a timer counting down from ten minutes.

"Nine thirty-seven," she read aloud, kneeling on nothing. Then she hopped down and approached Gundars, saying, "The Switchblade must have a self-destruct mechanism if the wrong code is entered."

"That *is* the correct code," Gundars insisted. "I witnessed Lt. Percy enter it himself, and start the plane accordingly."

Rachel was pondering that information when Gundars, with all the subtlety of a blood-starved vampire, clutched her by the throat; suddenly the animalistic cruelty, the inherent viciousness under the smooth facade, was revealed in all its ghastly glory.

"Fix the problem, Agent Wright," Gundars said, his face a mask of venom, his tone as smoothly sophisticated as ever. "That is, after all, what I hired you to do."

With a contemptuous push, the arms dealer released the traitorous spy, who paused to regain her composure, then nodded to Gundars, and strode over to Scott.

"The code has a shelf life, doesn't it?" she asked him. "It times out. . . ."

Scott was still on his knees, hands behind his head, the guard nearby still training an UZI on him. "Oh, that would be an interesting safety precaution, case it was stolen or something. That's a good idea, Rach— I'll be sure to pass it along."

Thinking aloud, Rachel said, "Washington didn't just send you to find the Switchblade, but to fly it home, as well. You're a pilot, after all. . . ."

"I'm flattered you know so much about me. I can just see you, after hours at BNS headquarters, mooning over my file. It's sweet, but sad, really."

She ignored this, saying, "You must know the correct code, then—the new code."

He shook his head dismissively. "I think you're giving Uncle Sam too much credit. The ol' Leafy Bug just has a few kinks in her, that's all."

Her face tightened into a vicious mask and she drew

back her right foot, in its rather pointed leather boot, and kicked him in the stomach—very hard.

Scott doubled over; he didn't lose his lunch, because he hadn't eaten any. Using zen techniques to banish the pain to some corner of his consciousness—and it wasn't working very well, frankly—he managed to look up at her and smile.

"Been . . . been a kick knowing you, too, Rach. . . ."

Her face flinched with irritation and she said, "I don't have time for your nonsense."

"That's the trouble. . . . You never did. . . . So, how much is Arnold paying you?"

"The code, Alex. Spare yourself the pain—you know very well I've mastered every interrogation and torture technique."

"Thing is, Rach, if I'd known you were up for sale, I'd have made an offer myself."

She kicked him again, even harder, in the side this time, and he was consumed by pain, or thought he was—when she leaned in, and slapped him with her .32 automatic, it turned out he could hurt even worse.

The blow jarred something—something in his eye. He blinked, and then he realized: *he still had the contact lens in!*

The camera-eye lens was still in his right eye, where he'd put it this morning, when he and Kelly had done their silly seduction ritual with this lovely monster who loomed before him now. But the BNS wonks had done such a good job, made the lens so natural, so undetectable, that he'd forgotten the hell about it . . .

. . . *had Kel forgotten, too?*

Was it possible his partner was wearing the receiving lens, that the fighter had also forgotten about their little stunt? Or, in preparation for the fight, had it come to the attention of his trainer or one of his assistants, and been flushed out. . . .

Rachel was calling to the floating partial pilot: "How much time left?"

"Seven minutes," the pilot yelled back, "five seconds . . . four seconds . . . three . . ."

"I get the picture."

Rachel got the picture; but would Kelly? Alexander Scott, hands behind his neck, watched as Rachel Wright motioned to a pair of Gundars's goons, saying to them in Hungarian, "Loosen him up for me, a little, would you?"

As the men lumbered over, fists poised, Scott managed to click a small button on his wristwatch, right before one of the goons launched a savage punch at his left eye.

In the process of winning his fourth round in a row, Kelly Robinson—in complete command of the fight, looking for the opening to put this second-rater out of his misery—suddenly saw a fist flying right at him, toward his left eye.

At the same time, Cedric Mills didn't seem to be doing anything but backpedaling at the moment.

Thinking the blow had connected, Robinson staggered on instinct, ducking way too late; and then realized no blow had actually struck him.

At ringside, the announcers were bewildered by this awkward lapse from the champ. "*What was that?*"

"Talk about a phantom punch, Bob! Robinson must be seeing things, 'cause Mills didn't even take a swing!"

Confused, Robinson was the one backpedaling now, trying to get oriented; and then more blows came sailing at him, and he did his best to defend himself, blocking this one, slipping that one, ducking frantically . . .

. . . while Cedric Mills stood, in the middle of the ring, well away from the seemingly shadow-boxing champ!

"Robinson is fighting—I just have no idea who!"

"Bob, this may be some new stunt, the champ's patented clowning—some more of his Ali-style rope-a-dope tactics."

"Well, there seems to be more dope than rope, at the moment!"

Mills, suspecting a trick, even a trap, nonetheless saw an opportunity and seized it; as poorly as the fight was going for the challenger, what did he have to lose? He went on the attack . . .

. . . and now Kelly Robinson was fighting two people at once, or was it three? One in one eye, two in the other, and in the confusion, Cedric Mills scored several big punches, jarring if not quite staggering the champ.

The crowd was on its feet—the tide had very unexpectedly turned.

"Mills scores!"

"Bob, I think Robinson's hurt. . . ."

Mills hurled another huge punch, sending Robinson reeling, his mouth guard flying in a shower of spittle and blood.

The ref jumped in, sending the fighters to neutral corners, while Jerry climbed up onto the ring lip to provide a water bottle for the mouth piece to be washed off, when the ref walked it over.

Now, finally, with a moment to think, to gather himself, Robinson realized he still had that contact lens in one eye—that he was currently monitoring his partner in espionage. Closing one eye, he viewed the scene more clearly, seeing . . .

. . . two thugs, holding onto Scotty! Then a woman in black whipped a kick at the spy, as if slapping him with the toe of her boot. Then she got right in Scott's face . . . which put her right in Robinson's face, too. . . .

Rachel Wright!

Leaning against the ropes in the neutral corner, his ring attendants all around him, Robinson said, "That bitch is *alive!*"

Sponging the champ's face, Jerry said, "Yeah, that bitch Mills is alive, all right—what the hell you doin' out there?"

Robinson, the scene of Scotty's torture vivid in his left eye, said, "No, man, you don't get it—the bitch is alive, and she's kicking his ass!"

"No," Jerry said, "the bitch is kickin' *your* ass."

Darryl, shaking his head, toweling the champ, said to T.J., "He's punch drunk."

To Robinson, T.J. said, "What's your name, baby?"

"Kelly Robinson. Fifty-seven and oh."

Shrugging, T.J. said to Darryl, "He's cool, man. He's got his marbles."

Jerry slipped the now-cleaned mouthpiece back in the champ's mouth, as the referee, centering, motioned to get it on.

The ref moved aside, and Mills charged in; closing his left eye momentarily clouded, if not shut off, the image being sent by Scotty's eye-cam, allowing Robinson to focus on Mills, see him more clearly.

And now Kelly Robinson had command of the fight again, throwing a torrent of punches that knocked the confidence back out of the challenger, if not quite knocking him off his feet as the champ had intended and hoped.

The ringside announcers were, like the crowd, out of their chairs. "*Kelly Robinson is* back!"

"*Bob, you have to wonder if the champ was just* playing *with his opponent, before. . . .*"

The cheers and excitement in the arena were both exhilarating and deafening, as Kelly Robinson threw everything in his considerable book at Cedric Mills.

From the champ's ring, Jerry—concerned despite the amazing comeback—yelled, "*Guy's a bull, Kel! Take your time!*"

But time was a luxury Kelly Robinson did not have—his partner, his friend, was in the hands of traitors and terrorists, facing torture and death. The fight Alexander Scott faced was life or death—not the entertainment of a mere sporting event.

Between flurries, Robinson said, "You need to go down *now,* Ced—and I mean *now* . . . don't make me hurt you."

"You can try, big man . . . you can try. . . ."

And try Robinson did, connecting a solid right with the challenger's chin that buckled the man's knees, following with a left hook that sent him soundly to the canvas.

Now the crowd did its best to blow the roof off the joint with their cheers, their screams, their whistles. No dancing, no showboating, no show business at all, Robinson watched, anxiously, as the ref flew and began to count the challenger out.

"Hurry up, man," Robinson said under his breath.

But when the ref hit the five count, Mills—*unbelievably*!—climbed back to his feet, obviously furious with himself, his self-anger fueling, firing him.

Robinson opened his left eye and allowed the terrible scene to play. . . .

On the bridge turret's deck, General Zhu Tam solemnly faced a frustrated Arnold Gundars.

"I mean no disrespect, Mr. Gundars," the general said. "I am sure we will do further business . . . but you must understand, no plane—no sale."

"Patience, my friend," Gundars said, with a strained smile, raising a hand. He looked toward Rachel, who hovered over a bloodied, haggard Alexander Scott, surrounded by men with the spy's blood on their knuckles. "My dear . . . you have six minutes. Use them wisely."

Rachel frowned at Scott. "You may not believe me, Alex, but I do have a certain affection for you. . . ."

"That . . . that mighta meant more to me, a while back."

"But now it's going to get ugly."

"Ugly? Not you, Rach . . . never you."

She shrugged, withdrawing a six-inch blade from her boot. "Messy, then. . . ."

"Rach, don't embarrass yourself . . . remember your BNS training. Push a human past a certain threshold of pain, he or she will lose consciousness. . . ."

She raised the blade; its sharp, shiny steel winked at Scott.

"Rach, if I'm unconscious, what good am I to you?"

"Any other point you'd care to make, Alex?"

". . . I guess not."

"Then let me make one. . . ."

And the beauty in black shoved the blade into Scott's thigh, about three inches.

Scott did what any well-trained, highly skilled secret agent would have done in his place.

He screamed.

Mills, having taken his mandatory eight count, came back at Robinson with renewed vigor.

From the corner, Jerry called to his man: *"Come on, Kel—scientific, son! Take your time! You can't rush a bull."*

The challenger was circling the champ. Robinson watched carefully, but both eyes were open now . . . and he could see Rachel Wright, twisting that knife.

And, champion that he was, Kelly Robinson knew what he must do.

Robinson may not have known it, but the one thing bigger about him than his ego was heart, his hero's heart.

The Middleweight Champion of the world glanced at his left shoulder—the bare one, the right cluttered with tattooed reminders of fifty-seven victories—and then he took a deep breath . . .

. . . and lowered his gloves.

Cedric Mills saw daylight and swung, connecting beautifully, perfectly.

And Kelly Robinson hit the canvas.

"Robinson is down! Robinson is down!"

Everyone in the arena stood, and a collective gasp went up, the entire crowd stunned, including the challenger.

The only one not stunned was Kelly Robinson, closing his eyes on the canvas, waiting for the count, taking the only dive of his career . . . in hopes of saving his friend.

12

··

Within Budapest Promenade Sports Arena, at the end of
the ten count, pandemonium reigned—cheers melded
with bellows of dismay into one huge cacophony, and
the only person not on his feet was Kelly Robinson.

Then the fighter got up, not at all unsteadily, met by
his trio of ring attendants, who seemed more bewildered
than disappointed. Elsewhere in the ring, Mills was
lifted high on the shoulders of his own crew, their man a
hero now, the new World's Middleweight Champion.

In his corner, Robinson commanded, "Cut the
gloves!"

As Jerry cut off the laces, T.J. leaned in, "Champ—
what the hell—"

"The mission, T.J.—remember? I'm needed.
Scotty's in trouble."

Darryl, at Robinson's other side, frowned. "The
white boy . . . ? What . . . ?"

"Listen, I need you to take care of those big chumps
down front—remember what I told you?"

T.J. was nodding, then so were Darryl and Jerry; no
questions now—they could read the demeanor of their
man, and knew this was serious, deadly serious.

Then Robinson bolted over the ropes, heading down the aisle, pulling off the gloves, discarding them, cutting through the crowd, who pawed at him, and called to him; but the fighter ignored them, and was unhampered by their efforts. His bearing was so grave, even the over-eager fight fans knew to give him space.

In the meantime, T.J., Darryl and Jerry were already blocking the path as the trio of burly Gundars goons sought to follow the ex-champ.

"What's up, fellas?" T.J. said.

The bearded bear in front of the slender T.J. looked derisively down. In a thick accent, he said, "Out of my way, little man."

Big Jerry had squared off with one who was only slightly bigger than himself, but small bald Darryl seemed hopelessly outclassed by his beast.

Yet for some reason, Darryl was smiling up at his looming gorilla. "Howdy, fellas," the bald trainer said. "We're Mr. Robinson's personal secretaries. You'll need to make an appointment . . . through us."

And the thug reached out to push Darryl, who—with a graceful form Kelly Robinson himself might have envied—slipped the blow and returned it with one of his own.

The crowd, at least those in the front of the arena, were then treated to another exciting fight—a bloodier, more brutal one even than Mills and Robinson had waged. The brawny Hungarian trio seemed to have the advantage—in weight, height, and reach.

On the other hand, the Hungarians weren't wearing brass knuckles.

*   *   *

On the bridge turret rooftop, Alexander Scott was screaming, as the woman he had loved twisted the knife in his thigh, tearing muscle, sending blood streaking, soaking down his pant leg.

"All right!" Scott yelled, apparently caving. "Okay—I'll tell you what you want to know!"

Rachel stopped turning the blade, but didn't withdraw it from the sheath of Scott's flesh, and her hand remained tight on the hilt. "Good."

"So . . . what . . . what was it you wanted to know?"

"Alex . . . don't push me. . . ."

"The code! Oh yeah, the code . . . well, it doesn't change, you know, doesn't cycle automatically in a different one. You *do* have the right code."

She frowned in confusion. "Then, why—?"

"The ignition has to be reset."

"All right, Alex," she said, with strained patience. "How?"

He shrugged. "Can't tell you that. Rach, you know information like that is strictly classified. Can't your ace pilot figure it out for himself?"

With an irritated sigh, she turned the blade, with all the emotion of a housewife tending a pot on her stove.

"*Ouch!*" He frowned at her. "Hey, that really hurts. . . . There's a green button on the left console."

She called to the pilot, whose head and shoulders floated above the invisible plane. "Green button! On the left of the console!"

Zhu Tam's flier frowned, hesitating. In Korean, he

said to his general, "Sir, how do we know the prisoner is telling the truth?"

The general said, "We have no better alternative. Do it."

After a skeptical lift of the eyebrows, the pilot pushed the green button.

"Something better happen," Rachel said.

"Something will," Scott said.

And the Switchblade's counter measures kicked in, a thermal flare used to decoy heat-seeking missiles firing out the back of the fuselage, sending flame streaking into the nighttime sky, an impromptu one-burst (but nonetheless impressive) Fourth of July-type fireworks display for the city of Budapest.

A few minutes prior to Scott tricking his captors into firing off that attention-grabbing flare, Kelly Robinson—watching as Alex was questioned and tortured by the beauty in black leather—took a quick detour through the lockerroom to throw on his clothes, all the while trying to determine the location of his partner's captivity.

He could not, after all, rescue Scotty without knowing where the secret agent was being held; it seemed to be an outdoor location, high up . . . a building's rooftop, maybe? What were those cables he caught sight of, now and then, in the background?

Seconds later—black leather jacket over black t-shirt with black jeans (as fashion statements went, this one was fairly obvious)—Robinson emerged from the sports arena, and quickly but thoroughly scanned the sky. He settled on that bridge, the turrets, studying those cables and the stone structure that seemed to mirror the background glimpses.

But the Chain Bridge was only one of seven such spans over the Danube, and even if this were the right one, there were still *two* arches.

Scotty—where are you? Robinson's mind screamed.

And, as if in answer, a ball of fire lighted up the top of the closer of the two arched turrets of the Chain Bridge. For just a moment, the jet atop that turret was visible against the orange and yellow and red of the flare.

Then the signal was gone.

But it was all the fighter needed; he was running, weaving through traffic, heading to that bridge, ready to save his partner.

On the turret's deck, Alex Scott was putting on a mock apologetic expression for Rachel and the rest, saying, "Did I say 'green' button? I'm sorry . . . my bad. What I meant to say was 'red' button."

Rachel scowled at him—not looking all that pretty, at the moment—and yanked the blade from Scott's thigh; the wound burbled blood, and hurt like hell. But he soon forgot that.

The blade the woman shoved into his left shoulder had his full attention, now.

Without knowing it, Kelly Robinson followed the same suspension-cable path his partner had, making even better time in reaching the base of the bridge turret, where a door awaited. He slipped in, and on the floor at the bottom of the stairs, he discovered the corpse of the guard, limp fingers half-heartedly hanging onto an UZI.

Nice work, Scotty, Robinson thought, as he reached down and helped himself to the dead man's weapon.

Then he headed up the long flight of stairs.

Rachel Wright withdrew the blade from Alexander Scott's shoulder; she hadn't shoved the knife in quite as far as with his thigh, so he thought maybe she was easing up on him, or possibly just getting tired. Maybe she was realizing he was just too tough, too smart for her. . . .

"Okay, Alex," she said, in a tone indicating she was admitting her own failure here, "I underestimated you. You're tougher than I figured . . . and smarter than I thought."

He smiled at her, feeling vindicated. "And just think . . . you could have had me."

"Oh the long sleepless nights I'll suffer," she said, and she placed the blade of the knife at Scott's waist, slipping the tip under his belt. "You know, if you'll remember our training, there's one thing that always makes a man talk . . . no matter how tough, how smart. . . ."

"Cutting his favorite Banana Republic belt?"

"You're two words off, Alex." With a jerk of her wrist, she snapped the belt in two. She slipped it slitheringly out of its loops. "You'll recall this scene from earlier in our little melodrama . . . but that was just a dress rehearsal. . . . Take off his pants."

Not feeling at all tough, or for that matter smart, Scott looked on helplessly, held by either arm by two of the goons, as another one stood at Scott's feet, with a hand on either trouser cuff. The captive kicked, and struggled, and when Rachel moved in threateningly, brandishing the bloody blade, she provided a hole for Scott to see Kelly Robinson slipping through the door onto the rooftop.

The nearest thug whirled to shoot at Robinson, but the fighter—an UZI in his hands—sprayed the guy with bullets, the noise echoing off the stone, sounding strangely hollow and small in the night . . . though to the thug, falling dead, they were large indeed.

Every man on the rooftop—and the one woman— turned toward Robinson, several UZIs, AK-47s and assorted handguns sending a storm of gunfire his way; but the fighter ducked behind the invisible plane, on its slightly raised platform, and took cover.

This diversion gave Scott the opportunity to head-butt the single man still attending him, grabbing the automatic pistol the thug dropped, in mid-air, and— holding his pants up with one hand, shooting with the other—made his way across the rooftop, as quickly as possibly considering his wounded leg, pitching himself behind the invisible plane and its visible platform.

Then the two partners—the two spies—the two friends—were at each other's side, firing at the bad guys who'd brought them here.

"All right!" Scott said. "You musta seen 'em, stabbing me, and punchin' me and knockin' me around— look what they did to my nose, man!"

Robinson paused between rounds of gunfire to have a quick look at his partner's face. "Your nose looks about the same."

"Well, thanks, Kel."

Robinson said nothing.

An intense volley encouraged them to duck back around the platform, both men keeping low.

"Kel—are you okay?"

"Hell no! I ain't okay—I lost my first fight."

"Lost? You?"

"Had to come up here and save your sorry ass, didn't I?"

"You . . . threw the fight? For me? Wow. Man—I am blown away."

"You will be, you don't keep your head down."

"I mean . . . what a gesture."

Ricocheting bullets sent them ducking down even more.

"Kelly, you know what this means, don't you? You and me—we're back. We're the same again."

Shaking his head, Robinson said, "I knew I'd live to regret this."

"Good. Keep that positive thought."

And the two partners in espionage, noting an attempt by some of Gundars's men to move down around the other side of the turret, threw a withering barrage of bullets their way, driving them back.

Scott and Robinson now found themselves below the plane, on its raised platform. From here Scott could make out a small bomb hanging as if it were floating, though in reality attached to the underbelly of the craft; on it were Russian letters that were all too familiar to the agent.

"Are you kidding me?" Scott said. "Thought we got rid of this stuff. . . ."

"What stuff?" Robinson asked, not liking the sound of his partner's tone in the least. "What is it?"

"Old Soviet bio-weapon."

"What? Shit! Now, we gonna get our asses contaminated?"

"Not for a while yet. . . ."

"Not for a—"

"It's heat-activated. Requires an explosion of some sort, which we won't have for, oh . . . five minutes and forty-five seconds."

"Try one of your foreign languages on me—English ain't trackin'."

"It's simple," Scott said. "All we have to do is hold them off until the plane blows up."

"Plane?"

Another flurry of gunfire winged and whanged their way, this time clunking, clanking against the side of the invisible plane above them.

"Oh yeah," Robinson said, and smiled. "The ol' Leafy Bug. Thought I saw her sittin' up here . . . but aren't we a little close to this puppy, if it's goin' bang and bye-bye?"

Scott shrugged. "It'll only hurt for a second, bro."

Robinson was pondering that—he had come here to rescue Scotty, not to die with him—when a screaming jet roar caught their attention.

Everyone on the rooftop, in fact, paused in their gun

battle to watch as an F-15 streaked across the sky, sil-houetted ·for a split second against the nearly full moon; then a sudden *boom* signaled the cracking of the sound barrier.

"What the hell?" Scotty asked nobody.

And now the night sky seemed empty again—nothing but stars and the ivory orb of the moon, and a stillness broken only by traffic noise below.

Then came a flapping of fabric—faint but distinct—snapping in the wind.

Gliding down out of the night, a figure in commando black—suspended from a black parasail—zeroed in on the turret top. Finally, Gundars's goons fired up at this sight, rather blindly, and then laser dots appeared on two foreheads, as if the Hungarian strongarms had suddenly converted to hinduism.

Like a gunslinger, the man in black—swooping down on the rooftop—fired one round each from an automatic in either hand, Beretta 93Rs with triple laser sights.

And a pair of goons went thudding down, one bullet between the eyes assigned to each.

Zhu Tam's men were having none of it: the general and his men went scurrying for the stairs, the pilot having dropped down off his invisible perch, trailing after them, almost comically.

Torquing at the last second, the man in black steered himself skillfully, landing right next to Gundars, parasail dropping neatly behind him, like Superman's cape. The invader stepped behind Gundars, somehow undid his flowing train with one gun-in-hand, and with the other held a Beretta to the arms dealer's temple, using the man's body as a shield.

The remaining Gundars goons were frozen, awkwardly, waiting for an order from their captured leader.

Carlos Castillo said, "Ask your men to lay down their weapons . . . please."

"This seems to be a trend this evening," Gundars said dryly, and motioned to his handful of surviving gunmen, who—after glancing at Rachel, nodding her reluctant consent—set their weapons down on the stone floor.

Robinson and Scott had stepped out from behind the invisible plane and its platform.

The fighter asked, "Who the hell is that?"

"Carlos," Scott said. "He's like the agency's superspy. Mac must have sent him to save our asses."

Watching as the superspy deposited Gundars to sit on one of those vents, Robinson said, "I don't need my ass saved."

"I know—guy's always, like . . . butting in. Undermining me and stuff."

Now Robinson shrugged, frankly relieved to have the weight off his own shoulders. "Yeah, but, as long as he's in the neighborhood, we'll let the man think he's bein' helpful."

Carlos called to Scott, in that mellifluous Castillean accent. "Alex!"

"Hey Carlos."

"I take it the Switchblade is in self-destruct mode."

"Yeah." Pant leg scarlet, Scott limped a few steps

nearer his fellow spy. "I kinda did a number on these guys."

"Proud of you, Alex," Carlos said, with a smile that Scott found just a tad patronizing. "If the clock's ticking, though—we'll need that code."

"That's right. Uh, watch out for Rachel. She's a double agent."

"Yes, Alex—I know." Tilting his head, his smile openly condescending now, as if talking to a slow child, the superspy said, "The code? Why don't you enter it."

Frowning (to Robinson it seemed damn near a pout), Scott said, "I was just about to do that." He glanced at his partner. "See what I mean? Totally undermines my authority."

"Yeah, nothin' more irritating than some prick with a big ego."

Scott let that pass, then went to where he knew the ladder on the invisible aircraft should be, confirmed that with his fingertips, and—easing up some on his wounded leg—climbed up toward the cockpit, muttering, "I'm doing this 'cause I *want* to do it. . . . This is *my* mission. . . . I don't take orders from anybody on my own mission. . . ."

Robinson was ignoring his friend's bellyaching, watching instead as Carlos strolled over to the beauty in black leather.

"Hello, Rachel."

"Carlos," she said, coldly.

The superspy placed the snout of one of the Berettas

under her chin, teasingly, almost stroking. "You've been a bad girl, haven't you?"

Frowning, Robinson turned and felt along the invisible aircraft, locating the cockpit ladder; he crawled partway up and said quietly, "Yo, Scotty."

Scott was in the cockpit, within which the console was visible—one of the technological wonders of the invention, enabling a pilot to fly the chameleon-like craft—and about halfway through punching in the lengthy sequence of numbers required to input the code.

"I'm kinda busy, Kel."

"Hold up a second—got me the mother of all hunches right now."

"Busy, Kelly," Scott said, frantically entering numbers. "Not now. . . ."

"Superspy over there? He's workin' with Rachel."

"Kelly, if I don't finish this very complicated logarithmic code in the next forty-five seconds, we're all going to blow up. And die."

"How'd double-oh big shot know the plane was up on this bridge, huh? And how'd he already know that Rachel went bad? Everybody else thought the girl was dead."

Scott hesitated for a split second as Kelly's words sank in.

Carlos had turned toward them, obviously wondering what the fighter and spy were talking about. "Alex! Clock is ticking!"

"Always butting in," Scott muttered. Then he called

out to their apparent rescuer, "I'm sorry, Carlos! He was in a fight tonight. Little punchy!"

The console indicated twenty-five seconds remained before the plane detonated itself.

Alexander Scott had a decision to make: should he allow the Switchblade to blow up, and guarantee keeping it out of terrorist hands . . . but also guaranteeing his own death and Kel's and everyone else's on the turret top?

Or should he finish entering the code, prevent the plane from self-destructing, in the belief that he and Robinson could prevail over Carlos, Rachel and the remaining gunmen?

Scott said to Robinson—pointedly, and for the benefit of Carlos, "Kelly, I'm really busy right now. I need you to be more respectful to my fellow agent. . . . Why don't you treat him the way your grandmother treated you?"

"I don't think we got time for me to cook him up some greens, bro."

"No—your *other* grandmother . . . remember?"

"Oh!" And Robinson hopped down off the wing and, throwing his highest wattage grin at the superspy, motor-mouthing as he strode up. "Man means my Grandma Ida. I thought he meant Grandma Bibi. Now Grandma Ida made some nasty-ass collards, but man, could she whip up a sweet potato pie—you ever have a really tasty sweet potato pie, Carlos?"

The agent in black turned toward the approaching fighter, training his guns on the man. "Hold it right there, Mr. Robinson, if you would. . . ."

With Carlos distracted, one of Gundars's gang went for a fallen pistol . . .

. . . but the super-spy was having none of that: Carlos whipped around, Berettas blazing, taking the man down, dropping him in a pitiful pile. The remaining Gundars goons went scrambling after their AK-47s, only to fall like dominoes under the agent's expert firepower.

Arnold Gundars himself, seated on a vent—out of sight, out of mind—seized the moment to go for a fallen pistol, on the floor near where he sat. With the gun in hand now, the arms dealer rolled and, with a self-satisfied smile, was ready to train his weapon on Carlos, when his target wheeled and fired first.

Gundars clutched his chest, blood oozed between his fingers, and he gaped in as much surprise as pain.

"There," Rachel called to the dying man. "Does that 'fix the problem' to your satisfaction, Arnold?"

Gundars—finished, all thought ceased, all motor responses history now, like his dreams of ever-expanding wealth and power—pitched forward to the stone floor.

This, however, provided its own distraction, and Kelly Robinson threw a lighting left, from the spy's blind side, and took Carlos down, sending him into instant slumberland, legs going out from under, and he folded up into an unconscious pile, dropping his Barettas, which made harmless clunks on the rooftop.

Rachel went after the Beretta nearest to her, but Robinson was on top of her; he struggled with her for it—her hands reached it first—and, like a kid sister fighting with her big brother over a toy, she whined, "Let go! Let go of it—I'm with BNS!"

"Yeah," Robinson said, "right," and snatched the gun from her grasp and pushed her rudely away.

Simultaneously, Alex Scott made his decision: he punched in the code, with only two seconds remaining, the computerized voice from the console saying, "*Self-Destruct sequence aborted.*"

Now that Scott had correctly input the code, the countdown ceased and the engine whined to life; the stealth device was disengaged, and the Switchblade revealed itself in all its gray-blue needle-nosed sleekness, its wings retracted right now, at only half their span.

Scott sighed, and jumped down from the cockpit.

Rachel was getting up, scowling at the man who'd shoved her to the floor—Kelly Robinson . . .

. . . who said, "I don't think so . . . stay put. You ain't goin' nowhere."

"You fool. . . ."

" 'cept jail."

"I'm on your side, I tell you!"

"Save it for those hefty prison matrons with the short haircuts—that shit may just work on them. They probably gonna love you."

"Wait a minute, Kel," Scott said, approaching. He stood a few feet from Rachel and studied her closely. "What do you mean—you're on our side?"

Her expression as intense as her features were lovely, Rachel Wright said, "We have suspected Carlos was dirty for months. Why do you think I got close to him? Mac had me pretend to team up with him . . . cozy up . . . so we could finally nail his lying ass."

"Whoa, whoa!" Robinson said, holding up his free hand in "stop" fashion. "This was just a sting? A scam?"

She nodded, said curtly, "Exactly."

"Then how come you didn't let Alex in on it?"

"Ask Alex—these things are on a 'need to know' basis. Besides, Carlos is insanely jealous of Alex."

Scott frowned with his forehead but smiled with the rest of his face. "He is? No kidding?"

"Oh my God, yes—haven't you seen it? If Carlos had suspected anything, Alex . . . you would have been the first person he came after." She stepped forward tentatively, close enough to put a gentle hand on Scott's shoulder. "And I couldn't have lived with myself if . . . if anything happened to you."

"You were worried about . . . me?"

The other hand went to Scott's shoulder, as she said, "Of course I was. Alex . . . you know how I feel about you. You could tell when we kissed . . . I know you could. I couldn't hide it."

"I felt it too," Scott admitted.

They seemed about to kiss again, when Robinson—the only one who seemed to remember that they were standing on a rooftop scattered with dead bad guys and a recovered stealth jet—threw his hands in the air.

"Scotty! Come on now! This crazy bitch stabbed you in the leg, what, ten minutes ago!"

Scott's eyes narrowed and he smiled sly, nodding. "Ah yes, and how 'conveniently' she missed all the major muscles groups. Accident? I don't think so. . . ."

Shaking his leg like a dog after urination, Scott displayed the dexterity of his wounded limb.

"Full mobility," Scott told his partner. "Do you have any idea what kind of pin-point accuracy that takes? . . . By the way, first-rate work, Rachel. Really excellent."

"Thank you," she said, returning his admiring smile, then adding apologetically, "I was a shade worried about the second wound. . . ."

"No, no—it was perfect." Scott gestured to his bloody shoulder. "It seemed so . . . real."

Robinson was shaking his head, astounded by this love fest. "Scotty, this is crazy! It's whack!"

Scott turned away from the lovely spy, giving his attention to his partner, for the moment at least. "Whack?"

"You blind, son—you are blind right now, this minute . . . *booty* blind."

"Booty blind."

"Yeah, man, it's like bein' snow blind or some shit. Only there ain't snow—just booty."

Now Scott placed a hand on Robinson's shoulder. "Kel, you don't understand the espionage game. Here's how the spy world works: there's agents, and then there's double agents."

"Right. I caught that."

"And there's double double agents—*fake* double agents." Scott shrugged. "Pretty standard stuff, really."

"Really?" Robinson said, maybe starting to buy it. He looked toward Rachel.

"It's pretty standard," she confirmed, nodding. Then she winked at the fighter, adding, "Just don't tell anybody."

From the corner of an eye, Scott noticed movement, whirled, and Carlos was rousing.

"Uh-oh," Scott said, rushing over.

As Carlos began to rise, Scott threw a roundhouse kick, which the superspy nimbly blocked. On his feet now, Carlos fell into a martial arts stance, and Scott followed suit, the two men circling each other, occasionally throwing blows, both deftly ducking them.

Robinson did not get into it: Alex seemed on top of things, and, anyway, Kelly needed to keep his gun trained on Rachel. He was not at all convinced by Scotty's confidence in the woman, much less her own claims of innocence.

Between blows, Carlos—outraged but also confused—said to Scott, "What the hell are you *doing,* man? You're a bigger imbecile than I ever imagined!"

"Jeal," Scott said, "*ous*! . . . The ol' green-eyed monster. . . ."

"You fool!"

Carlos, enraged, swung a blow so fast Scott could not avoid it; suddenly he was in trouble!

Robinson—Rachel Wright be damned—rushed over to his partner and stepped between him and his opponent, like a ref. "Okay, girls—all right. That's enough."

Carlos stepped past Robinson, however, ready to deliver a savage blow; but Robinson grabbed the man by his ponytail, a convenient way to stop him . . .

. . . or so it seemed: the ponytail came off in Robinson's grasp!

"A fake," Robinson breathed. "Scotty, this guy's just a big sissy man!"

Inspired by this revelation, Scott threw a punch worthy of Kelly Robinson, and dropped an already disoriented Carlos to the rooftop, once again. A piece of rope, nearby—from when Scott himself had been a captive—gave the blond spy something with which to tie up the groggy superspy.

Already half-hog-tied, Carlos came around and began to sputter, "Let me go! Let me go, damnit— Alex Scott, you are an idiot!"

Scott stepped away, admiring his work—the great Carlos tied up like a rodeo steer. "I don't think so. I think I was way ahead of you, my overrated former colleague."

"Yeah, man," Robinson said, joining Scott to gloat. "We're on to you, baby—tryin' to steal the Leafy Bug and shit."

Picking up on that thread, Scott said, "And all this time you thought Rachel was working with you. . . . Well, she was working with *us*."

"Us?" Carlos asked, eyes popping.

"Us—BNS. She was working for Mac."

"No," Carlos said tightly, "she was not."

"She played you, Carlos. Tell him, Rach. . . . Rach?"

But the beautiful spy in black leather had vanished as completely as the Switchblade, in full stealth mode.

"Whoops," Scott said. To no one in particular, he asked, "Have I been had?"

"Oh yes," Carlos said, taking his turn to gloat now, despite being tied up like a steer.

Robinson said, pointlessly, "She escaped."

Rather lamely Scott suggested, "Maybe she went to call in to Mac."

Robinson shook his head. "See, I told you—told you she was bad."

"Bad, like in . . . 'good'?"

"Bad like in evil."

Scott oozed exasperation, facing his partner, hands on hips. "Well, if you were so sure she was evil—why weren't you watching her better?"

"Well, 'cause you said she was good."

"What the hell do I know about it? I'm a blind man! Booty blind!"

"Quit blathering, you fools," Carlos demanded, squirming in his ropes, "and untie me!"

Robinson touched his partner's shoulder, spoke softly, so that only Scott could hear him. "Hold on—Carlos, here . . . he's still bad, right?"

"Bad as in evil?"

"Bad as in evil."

Scott swallowed. "I hesitate to say."

A voice spoke to them from Carlos's direction—only it wasn't the superspy: it was Mac, his words emanating from the incapacitated spy's wrist communicator.

"*Carlos!*" Mac was saying. "*Come in! I need a status report.*"

But Carlos could not get near enough to his bound wrist to answer. And in the meantime, Scott and Robinson had moved away a few steps, to confab.

Quietly, Scott said, "Okay, so Carlos is good."

"Pretty standard stuff, huh? . . . Should we untie the man?"

"Absolutely not—he's got a tenth degree black belt and a horrible Latin temper."

Carlos called out to them: "You are going to live to regret this, Alexander Scott! I swear to God I will—"

Scott withdrew a handkerchief from his pocket, heading over to Carlos saying, "Yeah, yeah," and then stuffing the cloth into the man's open mouth.

"Now what?" Robinson asked.

"Now," Scott said, already walking toward the visible Switchblade on its perch, "we go home."

Robinson ran a bit to catch up. "What about Carlos?"

"He'll be fine. . . . It's a beautiful evening. Nice breeze. No sign of rain."

"Just leave his ass here."

"His ass and everything attached to it . . . why?" Scott stopped to look at Robinson, at his side now. "You got a better idea?"

Robinson glanced back at Carlos, then admitted, "No."

With no urgency at all, they strolled to the Switchblade, Scott saying, "Important thing is, we completed the mission. We got the plane back."

Within moments they were in the cockpit of the craft.

"Then we're heroes," Robinson said, almost posing it as a question.

"Most definitely heroes," Scott said, in the pilot's seat. "Yes we are."

"Then this brother's gonna get his parade, after all. We gonna get *our* parade!"

Scott smiled mischievously. "We just might."

And now the world's middle-weight champ was

grinning like a happy kid. "Yeah! That is what I'm talkin' about. . . . Roll me through Hackensack in this beautiful bitch."

Scott—his smile still devilish—asked innocently, "Wanna see something cool?"

"Yeah. Sure. I am always up for seein' something cool."

Scott fired up the engine—the roar was at once vital and terrible, a tremendous noise. As if floating, the aircraft began to rise.

"Now watch this," Scott said rather childishly. "This is where the fun part of being a spy comes in. . . ."

"I been waitin' for the fun part, I gotta admit."

Scott tilted the nose of the plane down, and moved the craft forward, off the bridge turret . . .

. . . *and the plane began to fall!* Barely had the pilot cleared the bridge when the wild descent began, the instrument panel reading, *Hydraulic Failure.*

"This ain't *fun,* man!" Robinson pointed out, his eyes filled with the river below as the plane made its sharp descent. The fighter was holding on for dear life.

"I know!" Scott said.

"You're a pilot! Fly this mother! I thought you said you could fly this plane!"

"Most cases, I could," Alex said, at the controls, concentrating so hard veins were standing out on his forehead. "But we've got no hydraulics!"

"And we need hydraulics?"

"Oh yes. . . ."

And the river drew closer and closer in their view

until the water seemed to come up and grab them from the sky, the massive splash as close to a tidal wave as the Danube had ever come.

Before long a yellow raft popped from the water, inflating itself, waiting for two agents to bubble up to the surface, and climb aboard. Which they did.

Soaking, heaving for breath, Scott said, "Are you . . . are you okay?"

Robinson, also drenched, similarly seeking breath, managed, "*Hell* no! I am not okay. You just turned my parade offa Main Street and straight into the river!"

"It's not my fault."

"No shit?"

"No. Hydraulic fluid was drained."

"Well, did you check the hydraulic fluid, 'fore you tried to fly my ass into the Hungarian wild blue yonder?"

"Uh . . ."

"I didn't think so. Damn! My first mission, and I do everything right—everything! Now I'm not even a damn hero."

The raft was settling down now, the huge wave the plane had made dissipating into a memory. Not far from where they bobbed on the surface, another survivor popped to the surface—a yellow and black-striped canister.

"What's that?" Scott asked, frowning.

"Nothin'. Just some flotsam. Or maybe some jetsam. I mean, that thing was a jet, right?"

"Yeah, it was a jet, but that's not jetsam, or flotsam, either. . . . That's a five-megaton, heat-activated thermo-nuclear device."

"Say what?"

"A nuke."

"Come again?"

Scott was shaking his head. "Oh my God," he said, thinking it through. "If we'd crashed on land, not in the river? . . . That thing woulda detonated, killing . . . millions."

This ghastly thought only made Kelly Robinson smile: an idea was glimmering in his eyes. "So . . . Alexander Scott, superspy . . . *that's* why you crashed in the water. 'Cause you knew doing that, this baby wouldn't blow up."

"Well . . . maybe subconsciously I knew."

Robinson scooted over closer to his partner, settling a damp hand on a soggy shoulder. "Of *course* you subconsciously knew! Because if I have learned one thing about you, Alexander Scott, it's that you are a very subconscious kinda guy. You knew *exactly* what you was doin'."

Getting it, Scott also began to smile. "Yes! I think you're right. 'Cause to me, human life is the most important thing. Precious. Valuable. Reason I . . . *we* . . . take these dangerous missions."

"Hell yeah! Me, too—I was, you know, leaning in toward the water, usin' my weight—to help move the plane toward the coldness. 'Cause, subconsciously, I also knew."

"You have your own subconscious streak."

"Definitely. And I'm gonna call my buddy the President, and tell him all this good stuff. And we're gonna get the Medal of Honor for this, both of us."

"You think, Kel? Medal of Honor. . . ."

"Oh yeah. We're heroes . . . again."

Nodding, Scott said, "Yes we are. . . . That Medal of Honor, that would really impress Rach. I just wish she was here to help us celebrate our great victory."

Robinson shook his head, firmly. "You forget that bitch. That booty is sweet, but it's dangerous . . . and there's plenty more out there."

"Forget Rachel?"

"Forget Rachel. . . . Let me tell you somethin', Scotty—only one way to take your mind off a woman that bad. . . ."

"Bad as in evil?"

"Bad as in good. You need another woman, bro. Now, c'mon, think—must be somebody else on your radar. Some other sweet thing. . . ."

Scott thought about it. The raft was bobbing gently, lulling them both.

"Well," Scott said, "there is this other agent at the BNS."

"See. I told you."

"She's in weapons testing." Scott shrugged. "I never really ever talked to her or anything. But, man, is she sexy! You should see the way she handles a ground-to-air missile. Unbelievable. Know what they call her?"

"Tell me."

"The Archer."

"See, now you're talkin'. The Archer. I like that."

Scott locked eyes with his partner. "When we get back, maybe we could work that, you know, singing scam with her. Like with Rach?"

Robinson waved that off. "Naw! No way. You ain't gonna sing no more—you just show her what you got in your trousers."

"Yeah?"

"Sure! Just take out your Medal of Honor, bro . . . and then do what every woman secretly wants a man to do."

"What's that?"

"Some amorous shit. Bite her hard on the ass. Show her you care."

Alexander Scott sighed. "You really are a true romantic, Kel."

And Alexander Scott signaled for pick-up, and the two spies—the two friends—bobbed in the raft, enjoying each other's wonderfulness, waiting for Mac to send someone to rescue them . . . and hoping it wouldn't be Carlos.

A Tip of the Wing

....

I was a great fan of the original 1960s TV series, I SPY, created by Sheldon Leonard and starring the "wonderfulness" of Robert Culp and Bill Cosby. So it was a real treat for me to write this updating of the concept from the clever screenplay by Cormac and Marianne Sellek Wibberley, Jay Scherick and David Ronn.

While I make no pretense that the geography in this novel is at all accurate, I would like to cite several references, including *Hungary* (1990) by Tim Sharman; *Hungary: a Country Study* (1990), Stephen R. Burant (editor); and *Prague and Budapest* (2001), Fodor's 2nd edition (also, video version of same). In addition, various internet sites, too numerous to list, were enormously helpful.

Editor April Benavides provided her usual strong support, providing me with extensive photos of the production in progress; thanks, too, to my friend and agent, Dominick Abel. Weapons info came from Joe Collins (no relation); wardrobe reference was provided by Dennis Cockshoot; and my wife Barb made several library research runs that were invaluable on a deadline-driven project like this one . . . which of us is Alexander Scott and which Kelly Robinson, I leave for others to determine.